THE COLORS
OF THE RAIN

THE COLORS
OF THE RAIN

R. L. Toalson

 YELLOW JACKET

This is a work of fiction. Any references to historical events, real people, or real places are used fictitiously. Other names, characters, places, and events are products of the author's imagination, and any resemblance to actual events or places or persons, living or dead, is entirely coincidental.

YELLOW JACKET
an imprint of Bonnier Publishing USA

251 Park Avenue South, New York, NY 10010
Copyright © 2018 by R. L. Toalson
Yellow Jacket is a trademark of Bonnier Publishing USA, and
associated colophon is a trademark of Bonnier Publishing USA.
Manufactured in the United States of America   BVG 0818
First Edition
10 9 8 7 6 5 4 3 2 1
Library of Congress Cataloging-in-Publication Data
is available upon request.
ISBN 978-1-4998-0717-2
yellowjacketreads.com
bonnierpublishingusa.com

To Memaw and Grandad'n,
wish you were here

—RT

America preaches integration and practices segregation.
—Malcolm X

The legal battle against segregation is won,
but the community battle goes on.
—Dorothy Day

SPRING 1972

RAIN

Most nights
I sleep just fine
because most nights
it doesn't rain.

The last time it rained like this
we drove past that curve
Gran always called dangerous
and saw lights flashing red and blue
and people walking around
and a body covered
with a white sheet
that glowed in the dark.

Mama didn't slow down long enough
to look at the twisted car.
It was too dark to see, anyhow.
We didn't know who was
under the sheet, but Mama said
a prayer for their family
as we drove on by.

EARTH

Granddad came over last month
and planted cabbage, yellow squash,
peppers, and okra
in the little square of dirt
my daddy marked.

Me and Charlie
tried to tell him
we don't like cabbage
or yellow squash or peppers.
We didn't mention the okra,
on account of Gran's fried okra,
which is the best fried okra
you've ever tasted.

Granddad said those are
the only vegetables
that will grow in a Texas garden
this time of year.

He said, *You never know
when you'll need
something to eat,*
and he just kept digging
with his pale, spotted hands.

Granddad says
things like that
all the time.
Mama says he lived
through the Great Depression,
back when a whole lot of people
went hungry.

I watched him
the whole time he planted.
He looked a lot
like my daddy,
long legs folded up,
head bent so I couldn't see
the white of his hair,
overalls pulled tight
across his back.
He touched the earth
like it was alive.

NIGHT

The night my daddy left us,
after we drove past
that dangerous curve
and thought it had
nothing to do with us,
a black sky dropped
cold-water blankets
on me and Charlie
and Mama
while we stood
in the dark
trying to understand
what those flashing lights meant.

I didn't sleep
for twenty-seven hours.

BIRTHDAY

My aunt Bee
calls me Paulie,
no matter how many times
I tell her I'm too old
for that nickname.
John Paul Sanders, Jr.,
is my real name,
but Paulie is what
she'd called my daddy.

Tonight, she's brought us supper,
since it's Saturday,
and Mama works late
waiting tables at a diner in town.
She spreads it all out on the table—
greasy chicken and
mashed potatoes and
rolls so buttery
they leave gray rings
on the white bag.
She tears off the receipt
with today's date,
April 16, 1972,
Mama's birthday.
She missed the Apollo 16 launch,
just like she's missing supper.

Aunt Bee knows
Mama won't be home
until later. She says,
Go on, then, and I dig in.
Milo sits underneath the table,
his long pink tongue hanging out,
ears cocked toward Aunt Bee.
She doesn't like it when
we feed him with food
from our table.
She says it spoils dogs.
I slip him a roll anyway.

A chocolate cake waits for Mama
in the icebox.

DIVORCE

Aunt Bee's husband divorced her
a long time ago,
so she comes to see us a lot.
Sometimes she washes dishes
and sometimes she
sorts the clothes.
Most of the time,
she brings us suppers
she didn't cook.

When I asked,
Mama said that
Aunt Bee's husband
didn't divorce her
on account of
her not knowing
how to cook.

CHARLIE

Charlie's hung some lights
on the walls of the family room.
Mama won't like the holes,
but even I think the lights
are pretty.

Every other minute,
Charlie looks at the clock,
her white face glowing
red and then blue in the lights.
Shouldn't she be here
by now? she says.
She only works 'til seven.
Her voice shakes a little,
and I feel it shake my chest.

Once a parent leaves,
you wonder if it might
happen again.

She'll be here soon, Charlotte,
Aunt Bee says.
Mama says Charlie's
a terrible nickname for a girl.
I think it fits her just fine,

since Charlie's the only girl
I know who climbs trees
higher than me and
drives Granddad's tractor
and swims in a dirty pond
full of snakes.

Aunt Bee puts her arm
around Charlie,
and even though she's twelve,
Charlie looks real small.
Aunt Bee smiles at me.
You'll lead the song? she says.
She's asked me once already.
I think she's just trying
to fill the space where
Mama should be by now.

SING

My daddy used to sing all the time.
Mama called it loud and obnoxious,
but me and Charlie
loved to hear him sing.
He'd sing in the morning
when he turned on our light
to wake us up for school,
and sometimes he'd sing in the evening
when he turned it off.
He was a good daddy
on the nights he sang.
I try not to think about
the nights he didn't.

Your daddy had a
one-of-a-kind voice,
Aunt Bee says. *Lucky he*
passed it on to you.
She whispers the last words
like it's something great to sing
like my daddy.

He was in a band once.
That's how Mama met him.
He used to tell us the story

back when we all
ate supper together,
how she showed up
the night his band
was playing at a bar
and he fell in love
as soon as he saw her.
He'd always wink at Mama
when he said that.

FIGHT

I do know
my daddy liked bars
too much.

He was in a bar the night he left.
I heard Mama tell Aunt Bee
he was so drunk
he beat a man to death.
The man's friends chased him
around that wet, dangerous curve.
And when his car left the road,
they shot him,
right in the heart, three times.
I guess they wanted to make sure
he didn't get back up.

I wasn't supposed to
hear this, of course.
But nobody ever tells
me and Charlie anything,
so we've learned to listen
real good in doorways.

I never did hear why
my daddy fought in the
first place. I sure would
like to know that.

RUN

Mama walks through the door then,
so I don't have to
think about it anymore.
I break into song,
with the voice of my daddy,
and I'm halfway finished,
almost to her name,
before I realize no one else
is singing. Charlie's crying
on the couch and
Aunt Bee's walking Mama
to the chair right beside
my daddy's old one.
No one sits in
my daddy's chair anymore.

Mama's black eyes are shiny
and her face is red.
She leans her head
back against the chair.
Her brown hair's stuck in strings
across her cheeks.
Paulie, why don't you
go get your mama something
to drink? Aunt Bee says,

and Charlie makes a noise
that squeezes my chest.
Aunt Bee eyes Charlie,
then looks back at me.

But I can only see Mama,
looking like my daddy used to look
right before he turned mean and wild,
and I bolt from the house,
like it's a reflex,
door slamming behind me.
It's almost dark.
Mama doesn't let me
go out after dark.

But I just run.

Paulie! Aunt Bee shouts
from the porch.

I feel warm all over,
even though it's cool out here,
since spring only just began,
and I stop only to turn around
and yell, *I'm not Paulie anymore!*

I head toward the woods,
Milo's four legs keeping time
behind me.

She'll leave,
she'll leave,
she'll leave,
my feet say,
over and over and over.

I try to outrun
all the words
my feet say.

SHOTS

The day my daddy left for good,
we sat on our porch,
waiting for him
to come home
like he always did.
We watched for his
electric-blue Fairlane with
rusted-out doors
and a droopy ceiling,
and we listened for its tires
popping over gravel.

I played with Milo that day,
throwing a ball he'd
always bring back,
and Charlie rocked in the
chair Granddad made her,
and we tried not to notice
the sun setting.

The sky caught fire
and started fading,
like it knew what was coming
and wanted to get away.
And then all those clouds

rolled in real soft and quiet,
without warning,
and before we knew it,
everything around us
turned black and wet.
Mama packed us
in Gran's car and
took us looking,
even though she always
did the looking by herself.
Maybe she knew
what was coming, too.

Flashing lights were
coloring our driveway
when Mama pulled back in.

I've never seen Gran
and Granddad run
across the street
like they did that night,
Gran in her nightgown,
shaking in the rain,
shouting for her boy.
Granddad pulled her,

dripping, to the porch
and held her while
a different rain fell.
Mama stood alone.

I'd heard the shots,
right after the sky
opened up.

Mama says that can't be,
seeing as it happened
a whole nine miles
from our house.
But I did.

SCHOOL

Me and Charlie
went to school
four days after that,
on Friday, spelling-test day.
That week we only had
nine words instead of
the usual ten.
We've never had only
nine words.

I hate the number nine.
It means something
I don't understand.
Nine miles left,
almost home,
and then gone.

When I numbered my test,
before my teacher
called out the words,
this is what I wrote:

     1. My
     2. Daddy
     3. Isn't
     4. Coming

5. Home.
6. He
7. Is
8. Forever
9. GONE.

I know it was wrong,
but they were the
only words my hand would write.

The day after that,
Mama pulled me and
Charlie out of school,
on account of our
mental trauma.

She didn't say we had no
car anymore.
I think she was ashamed
of that part.

EYES

Daddy called his car
My Fair Lady.
Mama never had a car.
Gran told Mama
she could take us
to school every day
if Mama needed her to,
but Mama said
no, thank you.
She'd teach us herself
for a while.

Mostly she just leaves
worksheets on the table
and then forgets to ask
if we did them.

It's not right, those kids
not getting school learning,
Gran says.

I don't mind so much,
not going to school.
I never liked it anyhow.
But Charlie, she goes looking

for more worksheets
when she's done.

I don't want to get behind
for when we go
back, she says.

I hope we never
go back to school.

You're crazy, I say when she's
stacked more sheets on top of
the ones Mama left us.

Least I won't be dumb, she says.

Charlie has these really blue eyes,
like a clear winter sky.
My daddy had those eyes,
and they'd dance when he was
laughing and when he raged, too,
so we never knew
which one we'd get.

Will I be dumb
if I don't go to school?

Well, that doesn't
change my mind.
I still don't want to go.

FRIENDS

Josh and Brian,
my two oldest friends,
used to stop by after school,
and we'd run in the woods
together until suppertime.
But after a few weeks,
they stopped coming.

They live down the road,
not even half a mile
in either direction,
so I still see them ride by
on their bikes once in a while.
I can usually hear them coming.

I stopped shouting their names
after the fourth time they passed by
like they hadn't even heard me.

I reckon some kids think
a daddy leaving
is contagious.

MILO

I don't need friends, though.
I have Milo.

Milo isn't big, and he isn't small.
He has shiny black fur,
one blue eye,
and one brown one.
That's how come I knew
he belonged with us,
because he had
all our eyes in his two.

My daddy brought him
home from work one day.
He said someone dropped
him off and then just left.
I can't imagine doing that to a puppy.
Mama said we'd give him
a home for a little while,
but I knew he'd stay for good.

WOODS

I'm Milo's favorite person.
We wrestle and run together,
but most of all we walk
through the woods,
down to the dirty pond
Charlie jumped in once
on a dare.
Milo likes to swim in it.
That's one thing I won't do with him.
Snakes live in that black water.
I've seen them, heads bobbing
like little sticks,
only sticks don't float
and turn to look at you
and suddenly disappear.

I love the woods
because I can hear my daddy
singing here,
in the music of the birds,
in the music of the trees,
and in the music of me and Milo
crunching dried-up pine needles
under our feet.

I think he lives here now.

I haven't told Mama.
She would look at me
with those sad eyes,
and then she'd cry herself to sleep.

I don't like that kind of music.

So I come here
and let him sing to me,
like it's our secret.

SMILES

Milo gets silly in the woods,
since it's cooler under the thick trees.
It doesn't get too cold
in Houston, though.
It's mostly wet, heavy air
and hot rays of sun.
That's one of the things
I like best about it.

Milo rolls onto his back,
smashing needles and leaves
underneath him,
legs pawing the air.
I rub his belly,
and he smiles at me.

Most people don't know
dogs can smile.
Milo smiles at me
all the time, and I'm glad,
since I don't see
too many smiles anymore.

When a daddy leaves,
he takes all the smiles
with him.

LEAF

Come on, boy, I say.
It's getting close to dark,
and I promised Mama,
after running off like I did
on her birthday, that I
wouldn't stay out here
once the sun went down.

She's never said sorry
for coming home like she did,
tripping around like my
daddy used to do.
Charlie says Mama's
under a lot of stress,
on account of her job
and Daddy leaving
and the schoolwork
she has to make sure we do.
I think she adds
that last part to make me
feel guilty or something,
and it works, just a little.
I did my work today,
before coming out here.

I race Milo back
through the trees, toward home,
and I can almost feel my daddy,
running right behind me,
the way he used to.

When we're almost home,
Milo's feet uncover a leaf
shaped exactly like a teardrop.

I pick it up and stuff it
in my pocket
so it doesn't crumble.

Why do I pick it up?

I reckon it's like me.
Different from all the others.

I'm the only boy in town
whose daddy was a criminal.

SISTER

When I say
Charlie's eyes are blue
like a clear winter sky,
I mean it.

Josh and Brian,
back when we
were still friends
and I still went to school,
called her the prettiest girl
in the sixth grade.
I don't really know,
since she's my sister.
They'd talk about her
sunshine hair and blue-sky eyes,
and I'd tell them to stop being dumb.
They'd just keep talking.
And I had to listen,
unless I wanted to go
play all by myself,
which I didn't.

BRAVE

Me and Charlie
used to be real close
when we were younger,
on account of all the moving
and leaving our old friends behind
and making new ones every year,
but then we moved here
where Mama and my daddy
lived when they were
first married,
and we stayed.

Mama picked this place.
She said she wanted
me and Charlie to know
my daddy's family,
but I think what she
really wanted was help
with my daddy.

He hated it here,
with Gran and Granddad
right across the street
and Aunt Bee fifteen miles
down the road,

all these people
checking in on him
when he pulled in our driveway
too long after sunset.

The night my daddy left,
Charlie's eyes got real dark,
like a storm lived there.

Charlie loved my daddy,
even on the nights
he walked in the door
like he was trying not to fall over,
nights when he'd throw
ashtrays at Mama
and trip over chairs
like he didn't even see them.

Charlie was the only one
brave enough to stop him
when he turned mean.

CAUGHT

I shift in my chair.
I've been sitting for too long.
Aunt Bee turns on the water
at the sink, her back to me.
I stand, thinking if I'm fast
and quiet enough,
I might sneak out
before she turns back around.

Finish your work, Paulie,
Aunt Bee says.
Her eyes fix on me.

I'll do it later, I say,
inching closer to the door,
but she catches my hand.
Hers is small but strong.

Your mama doesn't have time
to make sure you do your work,
Paulie, Aunt Bee says.
And Gran says you run wild
in those woods all day.
That's why I'm here.
Sit down.

She sounds so much like Gran
that I sit back down.

Aunt Bee is nineteen years
older than my daddy.
She's short and wide
and starting to gray,
but she still looks young
in the eyes.

NUMBER

Mama's sending us back, Charlie says.

No? I say. It comes out
like a question.

Yeah, she says, and her eyes
tell me the truth.
She told me so last night.
Soon as fall comes
we're going back.

Fall is not far enough away,
and Josh and Brian were
my only friends.

When we moved here,
Mama said we wouldn't
ever have to start over again . . .
but I will. My daddy
fixed that real good.

I look down at my papers,
a whole stack of them,
with the number 9 skipped
on every page. I let out a

deep, long breath,
and Milo jumps to his feet
under the table. I feel him
brush against my legs.

I need a break, I say.

Aunt Bee pulls out a chair
and drops into it.
Her butterfly pin catches the sun
from the window,
and I squint against the light.
She shakes her head,
black-and-gray curls
bouncing against her face.
Your work, Paulie.
She taps the stack.
You're almost done.

She pulls one of the
finished sheets closer
and points to the number I hate.
You forgot this one, she says.
She flips the sheet over
and then looks at the next.

I don't answer because
I can see she knows now,
in the way her eyes turn soft.
Aunt Bee is smarter than
anyone I know.

Maybe that's why
I ask a question instead.
Will Mama leave, too?

It takes her a long time to answer.
She stares at me with Granddad's eyes,
and it's almost like she can see
all the way through to the
very bottom of me.
What does she see there?
She doesn't smile, just pats my hand.
Your mama won't do
what she did the other night,
if that's what you're asking, she says.

It's not what I'm asking,
so I say it again.
Will she leave, though?

Aunt Bee turns to the window
and stares outside.
It's a beautiful day, Paulie.
Why don't you take a break?
You can come back to all this later.
She stacks the papers up
real nice and neat.

It might have been better
if she had just lied,
because the storm starts moving
in Charlie's eyes again.

I push back from the table
and walk toward the door,
Milo beside me, and when
the screen slams twice behind me,
I start to run,
into the waiting woods
where my daddy lives.

APOLOGY

Mama stops by our room
on her way down the hall tonight.

Charlotte, go get me
some water, hon, Mama says,
and Charlie climbs down
from the top bunk
and is out the door so fast
I know they've planned it this way.

Mama sits on the side of my bed.
She taps the sketchbook open on my lap.
What's this? she says.

A shoe, I say.

She doesn't seem to notice
that it's my daddy's shoe
because she says, *Looks real nice,*
and smiles.

Mama hasn't smiled at me
since my daddy left.
It warms me all over.

Charlotte says you know, Mama says.
She brushes hair away from my eyes.
About going back to school.

What I also like about not going to school
is I haven't needed a haircut since I left.
My hair looks like my daddy's now,
straight brown strands that stop
right above my shoulders.

I'm sorry I didn't
tell you, she says.

It's okay, I say,
even though it's not.

I've learned that sometimes
it's okay to lie to Mama.

It's just . . .
Mama's voice cracks,
like the words are
hard to push out.
I don't look at her
because I know what I'll see.

Mama tries again.
I know school
was hard on you after . . .

I fill in the blank without
saying any words.

She looks at me,
and I stare back this time.
I just can't do it, Paulie.
I can't teach you both
and work, too.
She takes my hand,
and I know this is
her apology.

All your friends will be
so glad to see you.
Mama smiles again.
You'll be just fine.

I don't tell her about
Josh and Brian pretending
like they can't hear me anymore.

Mama stands and turns toward the door.
You can come back in, Charlotte, she says.
I see Charlie standing right outside the door,
looking like a shadow in the hallway light.
She hands Mama the cup of water
and climbs back into bed.
Mama stops at our door.
I love you kids, she says.
And then she walks down
the hall to her bedroom
and closes the door behind her.

SHOE

I'm not thinking
of school anymore.
I'm thinking about how a shoe
can tell a story, too.

He wore them all the time.
He was wearing them
the night he left.
I know because I saw one of them
on the television screen Aunt Bee
turned on after all those
flashing lights went dark.
It was a ways from his crushed-up car.
I reckon my daddy's shoes kept going
even after he lay still.

It wasn't the lead story
on the news that night,
on account of some space probe
landing on Mars without crashing
and my daddy's favorite musician
releasing a Christmas record.
Mars 3 and John Lennon's new music
were bigger news
than a man dying, I guess.

But the local station picked up
my daddy's story, talking about
the bar fight that ended in murder
and a car that lost control and
two men shooting the man
who missed the curve.

Why would two men
shoot my daddy
when he was already dead?

They never found those men.

That same night I heard
Mama tell Aunt Bee
that my daddy turned weak
a few years after I was born,
on account of the Vietnam War
and all those people
he had to kill.
She was crying
when she said it,
so I couldn't tell if she was
angry or just real sad.

STRONG

Mama called my daddy weak
for what he did.

We have this picture
of my daddy
in a uniform,
wearing those same shoes
he wore the night he left.
He doesn't look weak to me.
He looks strong enough
to save the whole world.

Me and Charlie never knew
the man in that picture.

Sometimes I wonder,
was it the war that
turned him weak
or was it us?

I close my sketchbook and
push it under my pillow
and turn toward the wall,
squeezing my eyes shut tight.

I'll let Charlie be the one
to turn out the light tonight.

SPOT

Today me and Charlie
do our lessons like we're told
and then Aunt Bee says,
How about we go to town
for supper?

Aunt Bee doesn't drive as fast as Gran,
but she yells at other people
through the windows.

Every now and then,
when she's not yelling at a driver,
she looks at me in the
rearview mirror, but I
don't look back.
I stare out the window,
watching the fields pass.
There's only one way to the
road into town, so we
already passed the spot
where my daddy
slipped and rolled,
which means I don't
have to close my eyes anymore.

DRAW

Haven't seen you
sketching lately, Paulie,
Aunt Bee says.

I draw in secret now,
after Mama and Charlie are asleep.
I don't want anyone to see
what has happened,
how I can't draw life
like I used to.

That shoe.
The broken stop sign.
Twisted metal that
used to be a car.

My daddy.

I draw what I see
when I close my eyes.

MAGNIFICENT

My daddy used to look at
every drawing I did
those afternoons we walked
in the woods.
Magnificent tree, Paulie, he'd say.
Magnificent leaf pile, Paulie.
Magnificent water, Paulie.

He called everything
magnificent,
and that made me feel
magnificent.

My sketchbook stays hidden
under my mattress now.
Every now and then Mama will
hand me that bag she made
for my drawing pencils,
and she'll say, *Why don't you
draw something for us, Paulie?*
But I never can. I just stare
at a page until she turns away.

LIGHTS

Aunt Bee pulls to a stop.
We'll eat first, she says.
Then we'll walk the springtime lights.
They won't be out much longer.

Charlie follows her
through the door of a restaurant
where me and Josh used to
get sodas when his mama
had errands to run.

We don't say anything
around the table.
Aunt Bee hardly touches
her food,
but Charlie eats all hers
and some of Aunt Bee's.

When we're finished,
Aunt Bee leads the way
out the doors.
Look at that, she says.

The springtime lights
are something special

this town does every year.
When we asked
Daddy if he would
take us one year,
he said they were
nothing special at all.

But they're the most beautiful
lights I've ever seen.
They hang from trees,
close enough to touch,
white-yellow and red
and orange moons lining
the path through town.

They're beautiful,
Charlie says.

Aunt Bee takes my hand
and Charlie's, too.
I stare at hers,
small and soft and cold.

Let's walk to the end, she says.
She buys our favorite sodas

from a little shop, and we
sit down on a bench.
I sip my root beer
and close my eyes.

WORDS

Paulie? someone whispers.
I look up.
Josh stands to the side,
his eyes on my face.

Josh, I say.
Maybe I just imagined
him and Brian passing by.

What are you doing here? he says
and looks around, like he's
waiting for someone.
His face is a ghostly white.

*My aunt brought us
to see the lights,* I say.

*Are you coming back
to school this year?* Josh says.

In the fall, I say.

His mama is coming toward us,
and I don't know how she does it,
but her eyes burn me
all the way through.

It's time to go, Josh, she says.
Her hand grabs his shoulder,
and she steers him away
like he's done
something wrong.

He doesn't look back
and neither does his mama.
But her words are clear.
That boy's daddy
betrayed his own people.
I told you I don't want you
around him now.

The world around me blurs,
liquid and hot.
I don't understand
what she means.

A hand touches my arm.
Charlie stands beside me,
that storm shifting
in her eyes again.
You don't need him, she says.
You don't need any of them.

Let's go home, Aunt Bee says,
and she takes our hands again.

Josh and his mama
are too far away
to see anymore.
But those words are
stuck in my chest,
like a bullet.

OUTRUN

The town smudges
outside my window.
I close my eyes,
my stomach clenching.

Aunt Bee drives like Gran,
fast and wild,
like she's trying
to outrun what
we all heard.

I sure wish she could.

We don't talk
the whole way home.
Aunt Bee doesn't even yell
at other drivers,
and for some reason,
this makes my stomach
hurt more.

QUESTION

Mama is sitting at the table
when we walk inside the house,
a plate of yesterday's chicken
on the table in front of her.

Did you have fun? Mama says.
I pretend she's talking to Charlie
and walk straight through
the kitchen to my room.
I hear her ask, *Paulie all right?*
but I don't hear
Charlie's answer.

PEOPLE

Milo raises his head
when I turn on the lamp.

Hi, boy, I say, and he
makes that little squeak
in the back of his throat
I've learned means
he's glad I'm home.
Milo doesn't bark.

My daddy said
some people just
choose not to talk.
I always loved
that he said people
and not animals.

We don't need words,
me and Milo.

ROOM

The last thing I drew in my sketchbook
was my daddy's messed-up car.

My fingers take over,
and before I know it,
I've drawn a room
I've never seen before.

What is it? Charlie says.
I jump. She sits down
on the side of my bed.

Nothing, I say.
I try to shove the sketchbook
under my pillow.

The page tears
from its spiral.

Did she see the whole room,
that white man on the floor,
the other men standing by him
and the blood puddle,
black on wood?

Does she know
I've drawn my daddy
and the man he killed?

Did she read the question
I wrote on the table:
Why would a man
beat another man
to death?

I'm really sorry, Paulie,
Charlie whispers so soft
I almost don't hear it.
My nose burns.

Charlie might be
my only friend in the world.

CHOICE

Charlie climbs up the boards
at the foot of my bed
and into hers.
She didn't close our door.
Mama's voice in the kitchen
joins Aunt Bee's.
They are talking quiet,
but we can still hear.

A new school
might do them good,
Aunt Bee says.
Let them come to mine.
They could start over
and no one would know.

Aunt Bee is a principal
at a big elementary school
in the city.
We celebrated real good
when she got the job,
being as women aren't usually
picked for things like principals.
I bet she's a real good one, too.
A little scary, but not too much.

A little nice, but not too much.

Things are just as bad
over there, aren't they?
Mama says.

I lift my head to hear better.

Maybe worse, Aunt Bee says.
I expect we'll have
some protestors.
Maybe violence.
Some white students
leaving the district.

Hundreds, you mean, Mama says.
It's happening all over now.
They're calling it
the new white flight.
I guess they think
schools with blacks
aren't good enough
for their precious kids.
It's real sad.

I have no idea
what they're talking about.

I know all that, Aunt Bee says.
But it doesn't matter.
There's a long silence
before she says,
It would give Paulie and Charlie
a new start.
No one would know
their white daddy killed a white man
to protect a black man.

The air is sucked
right out of my lungs.
I can't breathe.
I don't know if I'll
ever breathe again.

Paulie would never
agree, Mama says.

Paulie doesn't have
another choice, Aunt Bee says.
Her voice is louder this time.

She sighs.
I could pick them up and
drop them off every day.
You wouldn't have to
worry about it.

They're quiet
for a few minutes,
and then Mama says,
I'll talk to them.

FACE

My daddy killed
a white man
to protect a black man.
Did I ever really know
my daddy at all?

My heart beats
loud and hard.
My legs are too hot for covers.
I throw them off.

Mama passes by
and closes her door.
Charlie falls asleep.
But I stay awake for a
long time. My head
can't stop spinning.

I take out my sketchbook,
straighten my torn drawing,
and by the light of the hallway,
I shade in the face of the man
standing next to my daddy.

GRANDDAD

The morning is warm and wet.
Dewdrops curve across
the branches of the bush
beside Gran's porch.
The drops look like
glass tears.

Granddad is working
in his garden out back.
Me and Charlie
let our garden die when
we forgot to water it.

I'll share what I grow
in my garden so you don't
have to eat that trash
Bee brings over, he said
when he found out.

He only trusts
the food he grows or kills
with his own two hands.

I watch Granddad pick up dirt
and let it slide between his fingers.

He sits back on his heels and wipes
his hands on dirty overalls.
Granddad looks at me.
Why don't you give me
a hand, Paulie? he says.

I kneel beside him,
and we work together.
He tells me a story
of his railroad days,
when men laid miles
of track in a day,
and a story about Gran
playing the fiddle
while he played guitar,
and how he taught my daddy
and Aunt Bee to play guitar, too.

She doesn't
play anymore, he says.
Wouldn't even take
Reta's old piano we gave her.

Reta is Gran.

He says the last part
real soft, like it's just
a thought he didn't mean
to say out loud.

PLAY

Will you play me a song? I say.
I want to close my eyes
and see my daddy.

Granddad looks at me
for a long time.
His white hair, what's left of it,
shakes.
Then he turns back to the dirt.
*I don't think these old hands
could play anymore,* he says.
*You should ask your aunt Bee
to play something for you.*

Then he shoos me inside
to clean up for breakfast,
and I know our talk is over.
Gran will be in the kitchen,
flipping pancakes onto a plate.

But before I go,
I look at the dirt.
He's written a word:
Play.

I once heard Mama
say that Granddad
is a stiff man who can't hear
a heart's cry for help.

But I think maybe
Mama's got it all wrong.

My heart feels like
the bush I pass
on my way back up the porch,
like it holds glass tears.

NEWS

Aunt Bee hasn't laughed
since my daddy left.
She stands around,
looking out windows
or flipping through
news channels.
They are all reporting
about the new
Westheimer School District
some white people are trying to start
so their kids don't have to
go to school with black kids.
She shakes her fist and
talks to the screen,
and I'm pretty sure
I'm not supposed to hear
the words she says.

LAUGH

I heard Gran tell Mama once
that Aunt Bee turned sour
after her husband left her.

But Aunt Bee
never looks sour
when she laughs.

She has this laugh
that lights the day.
She laughs and laughs
until she quits
making any sound at all.
She shakes all that laughter
out into the world
so everyone around her
starts smiling and then
laughing and then
shaking, too.

My daddy used to do
all sorts of things
to get her to laugh like that,
and I thought there was
nothing more magnificent

in the world than my daddy
cutting up just so
Aunt Bee would laugh.

He would say, *Jesus, Bee,*
you're gonna hurt yourself,
and Gran would wag her finger
in my daddy's face and say,
Don't you take the Lord's
name in vain, you hear me, boy?
and Aunt Bee would just
laugh harder.

Sometimes Aunt Bee couldn't stop
once she got started,
and Mama would have to
pound her back and yell,
Breathe, Bee! Breathe!
and my daddy would
wipe tears, too.

NOTES

1. Mama chopped off
all her hair.
It sits in tight curls
around her face,
smelling like smoke
when she walks
in the door.

2. There's a bottle
in the back of the refrigerator.
Its level drops
every day.

3. Aunt Bee sits here
late into the night,
snoring in my daddy's old chair.

SUMMER 1972

PENCIL

The pencil I use
for drawing
got too small
last week.

I looked for another
everywhere in the house,
but I couldn't find one.
I did find six bottles
of medicine with Mama's
name on them, full
of little white pills.

Me and Charlie have done
our worksheets in pen
the last five days, and no one
has noticed. Mama never
looks at them anymore.

TRY

The school year is over now,
but Charlie says
we have to keep working.

I start feeling a little crazy
when I can't draw.
I feel the pictures
stacking up inside,
and they do funny things.
When I look at
the magnolia out front,
I see it in black and white,
like it's a pencil drawing
and not a tree.

I guess Charlie told
Aunt Bee about no pencils.
Aunt Bee walks in today
with two big bags
of art supplies.
Regular pencils, and graphite
and charcoal ones, too.
My lips smile wide,
like they are swallowing
my face.

She empties the other bag
and lines the table with
bright and dark colors.
Charlie picks up a red tube.
Paulie doesn't paint, she says.

Has he ever tried? Aunt Bee says.
I shake my head.

Well, why don't you try? she says.
She slides all the tubes
back in the bag and
starts toward the door.
She carries all those paints out back,
behind the house and the dead garden
and almost to the edge of the woods,
where my daddy's shed sits,
shining silver in the light.

READY

I haven't been in the shed
since my daddy left.
Aunt Bee stands at the door,
like she's asking
my permission to go in.

The light's on the left, I say.

Charlie grabs my hand.
She clears her throat. *Ready?*

I'm not. But I
follow her anyhow.

SHED

My daddy's shed is musty,
like rain has gotten in,
but it's neat.
Aunt Bee stands looking
at the walls, where Daddy
framed the sheets of his
favorite songs and tacked
posters of John Lennon
and Jimi Hendrix and
Bob Dylan.

No windows, Aunt Bee says.
Her voice is high,
like something is caught
in her throat.

She walks to a shelf
in one of the corners
and holds up
the light my daddy used
when he was building the shed,
so he could find the gaps
and seal them.

This might do
for a time, she says.

She plugs the light
into one of the outlets,
and the corner floods with light.

Aunt Bee sets the light
on the ground and then
takes a box from the bag.
It's an easel, and when
she's done setting it up,
she hangs a canvas from it,
then hands me the rest of the bag
and an apron.

Whenever you're ready, she says.

I am lost in the
smells of my daddy,
the dirt of the floor,
the wood of the walls,
the airy gaps of those places
we never got to finish.

I stand there for a long, long time,
breathing and seeing and feeling,
and when I look around next,
Aunt Bee and Charlie are gone,
and I am alone in this place
my daddy loved.

ART

Mama always said that
my daddy made masterpieces
for other people
but didn't have any masterpieces
left for us.

I used to watch him,
bending over cedar,
carving art into dressers
and chairs and tables.

I pick up a brush, and I don't
know what I'm doing or
how to even mix colors,
but I paint. And when
I'm finished, minutes or
maybe hours later,
I step back from the canvas.

I can't say what the
picture holds, except color.
Red and orange,
green and blue.
It doesn't look like
the death I expected.

It looks like a sunrise,
a brand-new life.

DARK

Dark falls like a curtain,
fast, thick, and unexpected.
I'm still in the woods
with Milo.

The one time I forgot
to get home before dark,
Mama was waiting in her
rocking chair on the porch.
She was so mad
she was crying.

The trees don't let much light in here,
even in the daytime.
The woods get real dark
once the sun goes down.
But Milo knows the way,
even if I didn't.
Which I do.

We race through the trees,
Milo keeping close beside me.
He stops every time
I trip on roots,
three times in all.

HAND

When I burst out of the trees,
a flaming sky burns my eyes shut.
I open them and stare at the cloud
that looks like a hand
holding a cigarette blowing smoke
up into the last of the day's glow.
My daddy's hand, holding up the sun
so there's just enough light
for me to find my way home.
I smile.

Then I look at the porch.
It's not Mama sitting
in the chair, swaying.
It's Aunt Bee.

My feet touch the stairs
before she says, *Your mama
told you to be home before dark.*
Her voice is soft,
but her eyes flash lightning
in the porch light.

Mama's not here, I say,
and it's the first time

I've ever said anything
like that to Aunt Bee,
being as my daddy
taught me better.
It's just that my insides
feel like a wild hurricane.

LOCK

Aunt Bee gets up
and walks to me.
She leans close,
smelling like peppermint.
Doesn't mean the rules
don't apply, Paulie, she says.
A boy could get lost
in those dark woods.

She wouldn't care, I say.
Aunt Bee's eyes narrow
and she steps back
and folds her arms
like she does when
she's real mad.

You better believe
she would, Paulie, she says.
Your mama loves you.
You think it's easy for her,
now that your daddy's gone?

I shake my head, but my
insides shake even harder,
since Aunt Bee is
chewing her lip.

She chewed her lip
when she told Mama
everything would be all right
the day my daddy
thumped into the ground.
She chewed her lip
when she told Gran
she'd talk to my mama
about our empty pantry
and then she filled it
herself instead.
She chewed her lip
when she told Charlie
my daddy wasn't a drunk
who chased women, like
my mama screamed down
our hall one night when she
came home tripping over chairs.

That's how come I know.

So I turn away from Aunt Bee
chewing her lip, and I walk down
the same hall where my mama
screamed those words,

and I slam the door behind me.
Hard, hard, hard, like I feel.

And then I lock it tight
so no one, lying or truth-telling,
can get in.

BREAKFAST

Mama stops by my
room this morning.

I would have kept the door
locked all night if Charlie
hadn't banged on it,
shouting that she
needed to sleep, too.

I feel Mama there for a long time,
standing over me, watching.
She bends close and kisses my cheek.
I pretend I'm asleep,
but I guess she can tell.
I know you're awake, Paulie, she says.
She waits, and I open my eyes.
Hers are dark and deep.
Want to have breakfast with me?

EMPTY

Me and Charlie usually
have breakfast over at Gran's now,
on account of our empty pantry
and even emptier icebox.

The other day, Charlie took
Gran's recipe for biscuits
from the book that sits
on Gran's cabinet corner
and tried to make some for us,
but when we opened the flour
from our pantry, it moved.
Charlie screamed and made me
take it out back and dump it.
I didn't tell her, but I gagged
watching that flour crawl
when I shook it out on our grass.

CUP

I follow Mama to the kitchen.
She opens the icebox and
stares at the only thing inside:
a bottle she must have
brought home last night,
since it wasn't there
when I checked yesterday.
Not much to eat, she says
and shuts the door.
She walks into the pantry
and comes back out
with nothing.

Her eyes turn watery
when she looks at me.
I'll call Gran, she says.
*She probably has
something cooking.*

It's okay, I say.
*I'll walk over when
Charlie gets up.*

She nods and turns
toward the cabinet
that hides our cups.

When she opens it,
I see my daddy's cup
way in the back,
behind two others.

No one ever drinks from that one.
She takes out two, careful
not to touch my daddy's,
and fills them with sink water.
Then she carries them
to the table and sets one
in front of me.

MAMA

When she's standing or sitting
or sleeping, it's hard to tell
how Mama is vanishing.
But when she's walking,
when her stick-legs start moving,
I see the bones knocking
against clothes that sag
and bunch.

*I'm not doing too well
since your daddy . . .* she says,
but I guess she can't
say all the words.
She stares at her fingers,
spread out on the table
in front of us.
Her nails are
black and dirty.

It's all right, I say again,
even though it's not.

She plays with an
imaginary line on the table.
I watch her hands

with scratches and spots
I don't remember.

I'm sorry, she says,
and this time she
looks right at me.
For a minute, I look back.
Her eyes wrap around me.

Mama is supposed to know
the right way from here,
what to do and how to live
without my daddy,
but she looks at me
like maybe I'm the one
with all the answers.

I look away, and Mama
squeezes my hand,
like she's saying
she understands.
I love you, Paulie, she says.

SUMMER

Bee wants to take you and Charlotte
this summer, Mama says.
There's something I gotta do.
She looks at me,
like she's trying to make me
understand, but I don't.
She's leaving us, too, then.
The hole in my chest widens.
I can't say a word.
Mama's quiet for a minute,
and then she says, *I'll sure*
miss you both. But Bee's
a good woman. Always was.
The silence moves around us,
like that flour in its bag.
She'll take good care
of you.

She stands and crosses the floor
to dump what's left of her water
back in the sink, and then she
stoops to kiss my hair.
I have to go to work, Paulie, she says.
I enjoyed breakfast.

I reckon she forgot
we didn't eat anything.

She's gone before I can say
I love her, too.
So I chase her out the door
and yell it into the morning.

She smiles and
climbs in Gran's car.
She drives off
without looking back,
even though I'm waving
from the porch.
And I'm a little bit glad,
since now she won't see me cry.

SUPPER

I spend all day
walking the fields,
trying to find just
the right flowers
for our table.

It's our last night at home,
and Charlie cooked Mama's
favorite supper.
Gran's car pops into the drive,
and I yell to Charlie,
loud as I can, *She's here!*
and race through the door
and into the kitchen,
where I see the rest of my flowers
sitting in the middle of the table,
arranged in a way that
makes them look like more
than the wildflowers they are.

Charlie hands me a plate,
piled high with steaming
hot chicken potpie
I didn't even know
she could make.

Green beans and corn
and carrots spill out
the sides in a soupy sauce
I can't wait to taste.

CLOUD

The screen door slams,
and by the time Mama
moves into the room,
me and Charlie are
waiting for her.
I'm trying not to notice
how good the food smells,
trying to wait for everyone
to sit down before I put
a single bite in my mouth.

Hurry, hurry, hurry,
my stomach says.

Charlie waves at the plate
in front of an empty seat.
I cooked, she says.
Her face glows bright.

Mama's smile shakes.
She stares at the plate we've
set for her, and she hesitates.
Me and Charlie notice,
and the air around the table
turns thick and dark,

like a rain cloud followed
Mama in.

Then Mama sits.
Thank you, hon, she says.

We eat in silence,
both of us watching Mama
picking at her food.
Every now and then
she puts a carrot
in her mouth,
but nothing else.

I look at Charlie.
Her eyes are
wet storms.

TIRED

I want to tell Mama
it's our last night,
that I picked all these
flowers for her,
that Charlie spent
a whole hour cooking
this meal. But the only thing
that comes out is
I love you, Mama.

Mama looks at me for a minute,
and then she smiles on her face
but not in her eyes.
I love you, too, she says.
She puts down her fork.
I know it's your last night home.
She lifts one shoulder,
like she's not sure she
should say more. But she does.
It's just that I'm tired.

And then she's standing,
pushing in her chair.
It scrapes the floor like
her words scrape us.

I stare at her face, at those
dark eyes that look emptier
than I've ever seen them,
even on the morning
after my daddy left.

Thank you for dinner, she says,
turning so she can walk
all the way down the hall
and into her room,
where she'll spend the rest
of this last night home
locked away from us.

MISS

Charlie glances at the Monopoly box
she set on the counter
right before supper and then
looks down at her plate,
almost empty. I wonder
if she feels as sick as I do.

She stands and carries her plate
and Mama's still-full one
to the sink.
I follow her with mine. I'm about to
turn toward our room when Charlie
grabs my arm. She's holding
out the box.

Want to play Monopoly?
she says, her eyes
almost clear again.

I nod, and we spread the board
across the table and play
until it's so late our eyes
start sliding closed,
hours and hours of
pretending we didn't

need Mama for this fun,
pretending we don't care
that she chose her room
over us, pretending we're not
thinking about how
we'll miss her in a way
she won't miss us.

HOME

Aunt Bee comes for us early.
Mama is already gone.
All ready to go? Aunt Bee says,
eyeing the suitcases
piled in the living room.
She only lives across town,
but me and Charlie packed
about everything we owned,
except for our winter clothes.

We still don't know
what we'll be doing
at Aunt Bee's house
or how long we'll stay.

Aunt Bee picks up two bags,
and me and Charlie carry the rest.
Don't worry about art supplies, Paulie.
The bags smack her legs.
I have plenty.

I grab my pencil
and sketchbook anyhow,
but I leave all the rest.
Milo jumps in the back seat.

Even though she doesn't like dogs,
Aunt Bee is letting Milo come with us.
I hugged her neck
when she told me.
I love Milo.
I didn't know if I could
leave him behind, and I
guess Aunt Bee knew that.

He'll have to wear a collar
and a leash at Aunt Bee's house,
but I don't think he'll mind,
seeing as it's the only way
we could be together.
Milo understands
things like that.

Let's go home, Aunt Bee says,
like her home has always
been our home, waiting for us.

PORCH

It doesn't take us long
to get there. It's about
the nicest house I've ever seen,
a neat garden out front,
no paint chipping on the sides,
a door you don't have to pry open.

Aunt Bee takes us right through
the inside and out to the back.
I look around her porch.

There's a back door painted red,
like the favorite shirt
my daddy always wore,
like Aunt Bee's face
those days he made her laugh,
like the stop sign his car
broke from the ground.

A green hose wrapped
around a hook beside the door,
like the one my daddy used
to water our garden,
like the grass in the woods
where he used to live,

like the old tractor he drove
for Granddad when Granddad's
arthritis kept him in bed.

A mop against a rail,
like the one my daddy used
to clean up the milk
I'd spill sometimes,
the one he'd hold
while he danced around
the living room just to be silly,
the one Charlie used
at Halloween one year
when we couldn't find
the broom and my daddy said
she could fly a mop instead.

Everything on Aunt Bee's
back porch reminds me
of him.

GLAD

Let him go, Paulie,
Aunt Bee says, and
at first I think she's
talking about my daddy.
But then I notice Milo
trying to jump right
out of my arms.
I set him down.

We watch him sniff the plant
growing up the side of Aunt Bee's
house. He lifts his leg.
I wonder if Aunt Bee
will stop him, but she doesn't.
When he's finished,
he runs into the grass
and collapses, rolling
all over it, looking like my
daddy's car must have looked,
feet, back, feet, back, feet, back.
Except he rolls one more time
so he can stand and then races
to my side so he can
lick my hand.

Milo runs back and forth,
back and forth, and I hear
myself laugh at the crazy of it.
That makes Aunt Bee laugh,
and Charlie, too.

The way Aunt Bee's
eyes shine and twirl
from me to Charlie
and back again
makes me think
she's saying something
I haven't heard in too, too long.

I'm so glad you're here.

NAME

There's a picture
hanging in the room
where I sleep at
Aunt Bee's house.
At first I thought it
was a real picture,
being as it's perfect,
with palm trees standing tall
against a blue-and-yellow sky.
But then I looked closer,
and I noticed it's a painting
that looks just like a picture.

I know because I found
a *BA* in the corner,
hidden in some twisted
tree branches so you
wouldn't see it unless
you were looking
really, really close.

I think it might
stand for Aunt Bee,
since her name is
Beatrice Adams.

I've found BA
painted into the corners
of other pictures
in her house, too.
But she's never said
anything about painting before.
I think she's trying to hide it.
I don't know why.

So today, when she leaves
to check the mail and pick up
our supper, like she does
every Wednesday, I plan to sneak
into her room.

LETTERS

Aunt Bee doesn't let
anyone go in her room,
not even Charlie, even though
Charlie is supposed to be
helping clean her house.
Aunt Bee says she cleans it herself,
but I can tell as soon as I walk in
that she doesn't,
being as the tables beside
her bed and the dresser
along the side wall hold dust
as thick as my fingertip,
like our tables at home
always did.

Lotion and makeup and perfume
are stacked all over her bathroom counter,
on top of some spilled powder
she must have never wiped up,
since it looks old and permanent.
Her bedsheets are tangled,
and a blanket is almost falling off
onto the floor.
The purple slippers beside her bed
are the only neat thing in the room,

looking like she just
stepped right out of them
and now they're waiting
for her to come back.

A curtain closes off
a corner of Aunt Bee's
bedroom, where the light
from two windows is
glowing through the fabric.
Something is there.
I pull the curtain back.

Out of the corner of my eye,
I see a chair and a table
spread with paint
and a stack of paintings
leaning against the wall
under the windows.
But I don't look at any of them,
just the one resting on the easel.
Sunbeams point to it, even though
the shades are drawn.

My daddy's eyes
stare back at me.

BA is easier to find
on this one, right across
the bottom in loopy letters.

CURTAIN

What are you doing in here, Paulie?
Charlie says, and then she stops,
her mouth open wide.

Neither of us says a word.
We just stare at our daddy,
looking real on canvas.
After a while, Charlie says,
We should get out of
this room. Aunt Bee will be
back any minute, and she
pulls the curtain back in its place,
hiding this corner
of Aunt Bee's room again.

SECRETS

Me and Charlie sit on the couch,
waiting for Aunt Bee
to get back home,
and I only think
of three things.

1. Aunt Bee is
an artist, a real one.

2. She didn't tell me.

3. What other secrets
does Aunt Bee have?

QUESTION

When Aunt Bee gets back home,
she calls us to the supper table.
Her house is fancier than ours
but not as clean. Papers are
stacked in every corner
of the room, and Aunt Bee
puts more on the pile
closest to her before
sitting down with some
fried chicken.

Mama would hate
this room.

It doesn't seem to bother
Aunt Bee, though, being as
we still eat every meal here.

I look around the room
while we eat, and I don't
know why I've never noticed
it before, but there's another
painting that looks like a picture
on the wall beside me.

It has the same palm trees
in the background,
and lights glow in the street
and on a diner
and on the hoods
of old cars.

I point to the picture.
Did you paint that? I say.
Charlie kicks me under the table,
but I hardly feel it,
since my whole body
is already burning.

Aunt Bee looks at me
with wide eyes, like she's
surprised. She stares at her plate,
but not before her eyes move
to the picture so fast I almost
miss it.

She doesn't say anything,
so I say, *I found a BA*
on the picture in my room.
I thought BA might be you.

I watch her face. She takes
a long breath, and then she
lets it out real slow, like she's
trying to think hard about
what she's going to say next.

That's what my daddy
used to do when Mama
asked him where he'd been
the nights he came home late.

Gran's coming tomorrow, she says,
and I know she's trying to
avoid answering my question.
She looks at Charlie.
*She'll give you a lesson
while she's here.*

Charlie takes violin lessons
from Gran. She's not very good yet.
She doesn't have her own violin,
and Gran keeps hers at her house.

I bite my lip, staring at the
empty mashed-potato carton.

My stomach turns over and over.
I reckon there are too many secrets here,
just like at home.

SURPRISE

I picked some things up
at the store for you both,
Aunt Bee says,
turning to me.
I don't care.
I don't care a bit.

But when I look at her face,
she's smiling so big you'd think
she just said my daddy was
coming back home. I feel my
mouth smile, too, even though
I don't want it to. It's just that
when Aunt Bee smiles, it's real hard
not to smile right back.

If you're finished,
I'll show you, she says.
I don't feel hungry anymore,
so I push my supper away.
We leave the food on the table
and follow Aunt Bee
into her living room,
where bags wait on her couch.

Aunt Bee digs inside
one of the bags and pulls out
a black case, which she opens.
She pulls out a shiny brown violin
and turns to Charlie.
It's yours, if you want it.

Charlie smiles so wide
the secrets don't mean
so much to me anymore.

Aunt Bee shakes out another bag
in my direction. It's filled with
canvases and sketchbooks
and more pencils than I'll ever use
in a lifetime. *So you can practice
your art,* she says.
My chest burns.

Me and Charlie lunge at Aunt Bee,
almost knocking her off her feet.
She laughs long and loud,
and I hear love all through the laugh
that shakes itself out into silence,

like it used to
when my daddy acted the fool.

Love lives here,
even in the secrets.

GARDEN

Every other week,
after Charlie's violin lessons,
Gran helps me weed
Aunt Bee's flower beds.

Gran says Aunt Bee was never
a garden kind of person, but her
husband was, and that's why
these beds are full of
so many dead plants.

I reckon Aunt Bee let them die
when her husband left.
I reckon I would have, too.

Gran says the plants aren't
really dead, they just need loving care.
She must have a gift
for dying things,
since some green is coming back.

LOVE

Usually, when me and Gran weed,
we talk about safe things,
like the weather and
what me and Charlie are doing
to keep ourselves busy this summer
and what Aunt Bee is feeding us
in place of Gran's Thursday night meat loaf
and Sunday afternoon pot roast.

But today she's brought up
Aunt Bee's husband who left,
and since I've never met him,
I say, *What was he like?*

Gran looks at me, her face
turning from bright red to a
pale gray, a shadow I can't read.
Then she looks down at the gloves
that carry dirt so her hands
don't have to. *Bee should never
have married him,* she says.

Why? I say. I just
can't help myself.

Gran pulls weeds out by their roots,
one after another.
It doesn't work that way for me,
on account of stems breaking
before the roots come loose.
Gran says it's important to get them out
her way, or else they'll come right back,
but it's not as easy
as she makes it look.

She keeps pulling, and I keep waiting,
thinking maybe she didn't hear me.
Then she wipes her hands on
the apron she tied around her dress
and says, *The only thing he was good for
was growing flower gardens,
painting pretty pictures,
and breaking hearts.*

He was a painter? I say.

A good one, Gran says.
*Problem was, painting was
more important than his family.*

You mean Aunt Bee, I say.

Gran looks at me for a minute
but doesn't say anything else.

So I say, *But they loved
each other, right?* since
that's why people get married.

Gran laughs, but it's heavy.
*Love had nothing to do with
that wedding.* Gran says it in a whisper,
and she looks real quick at Granddad,
sitting on Aunt Bee's porch,
rocking in a white chair.

So if people don't get married
on account of love,
then why do they get married?

Gran pats my knee with her
dirty glove and says, *Love is
a strange thing, Paulie.
It's a lot like a flower.*

She touches a plant that
looks greener than it did
the last time we weeded.
Sometimes it shows up, like a bloom,
after a person gets married.
Sometimes it's there at the beginning
and then it leaves for good.
She stares at Aunt Bee's house,
like she can see inside.
Sometimes it never shows up at all.

I don't ask her which one it was
for Mama and my daddy.

FLOWER

I move on, weeding
all the way around the front.
Gran works close beside me.

When we get to the
side of the house, Gran says,
Well, look at that. She's pointing
at a tiny white flower,
yellow tips sticking out
from its center.
Our first flower.
A beeblossom.

I don't think. I break off
the bloom and race inside
and push it in Aunt Bee's face
so she can see that her garden
is blooming again and it has
nothing to do with the man
who broke her heart.

Aunt Bee stares at it a minute, two, three,
and just when I think maybe I've done
exactly the wrong thing,
she takes it from me and puts it

under her nose and
breathes deep and long.
A smile squeezes out words.
*I haven't seen one of these
in years,* she says.

*All your flowers are
coming back to life,* I say,
and the words feel true.

Aunt Bee smiles real big then,
and it glows brighter than the
white flower in her hand.
Yes, she says. *They are.*

And then she tucks the flower
behind her left ear and pulls me
into arms that feel soft
and warm and safe.

FORGOTTEN

Three weeks without a call
or a visit or even a letter
from Mama, and we give up.

Maybe she forgot about us,
or maybe she doesn't
want us anymore, but it's
just easier to think that
we don't need her, seeing as
Aunt Bee is our mama now.

Aunt Bee would make
a good mama. We've found out
she can cook nearly everything
Gran's ever cooked, except with
a little more salt, and she buys
me new art supplies when my
old ones run out, and she takes us
shopping for new school clothes.

CALL

Gran called Aunt Bee yesterday.
Me and Charlie listened in
on Aunt Bee's end of the conversation,
even though she tried
real hard to talk soft.

She even turned around
a few times, to make sure
we weren't there, but she
couldn't see us from
where she was sitting.

We were there, hiding
behind the candy table,
where Aunt Bee keeps her
chocolate-covered caramels
and her orange wedges
covered in sugar.
And from where we hid
we heard words like *addicted*
and *how long* and *which facility,*
and I don't know about Charlie,
but now I'm more confused
than ever.

I wish I could have seen
what Aunt Bee drew
on the pad beside the phone,
but she tore it up after
she hung up.

TRIP

Today Gran comes to pick us up,
and on the highway home, she tells us
how Mama is taking a trip
for a few weeks
but will be back soon,
how this trip will be good
for her and good for us, too,
how we're going to eat
one last supper together
before she leaves on her trip.

Like a send-off party, Gran says,
except it doesn't feel much
like a party, since any way
you put it, Mama is leaving us.

DAY

Gran puts a silver pot
and a bright orange bowl
on the table while Charlie
sets out the plates and spoons.
Then we all sit in our places
and wait for Mama to show up.

We wait and wait and wait,
trying not to stare at the empty seat,
until Gran says, *I'll just go next door
and tell her it's ready,* and then
there are two empty seats.

I watch steam curl
above the buttermilk biscuits
we helped Gran cut out
with the top of a glass.
The best fried okra in Texas
is getting soggy in a bowl.

She's not coming, I say.

Charlie narrows her eyes at me,
like I've said something wrong
instead of something true,

but Granddad lets out a long breath
like he knows it, too.
He takes my hand in one of his
and Charlie's in the other.

Sadness can do strange things
to people, he says. *But your*
mama loves you.
And then
he says it again, in case we
didn't hear him, I reckon.
Your mama loves you.
And she loved your daddy.
His . . . He doesn't finish his thought,
just starts another.
It's been hard on all of us,
but especially your mama.

But he doesn't know the way
my daddy left that morning,
in a rage that turned his face
purple and his mouth
more than mean.
How Mama yelled back
until her voice just stopped

and the tears wet her cheeks
like the rain wet us that night.
How my daddy never looked back
when he spun the wheels and the
rocks spit in Mama's face,
scratching her cheek like she
needed scars more than
his staying.

Maybe they loved
each other before,
but I don't reckon
they did that day.

EAT

Granddad is watching my face.
I swallow the day and night
stuck in my throat.
He pats my hand again,
the tips of his fingers rough
and calloused.

Sometimes the way people
love us is hard to see, Granddad says.
It can be like a fire,
and we feel it burning all around.
Or it can be like a star,
and the only way we can see it
is by looking real hard for it
in the dark.

I don't know if I've ever heard
Granddad say as many words
as he's said tonight.

Granddad leans back in his chair
just as Gran walks into the room,
like their moves are a dance
perfectly timed. She looks at him
and gives a tiny little head shake,

no words, but Granddad understands.
He spreads his hands
and says, *Let's bless this*
feast your gran made.
So we do. And we eat it.
Without Mama.

STAR

Granddad's only a railroad man,
but his words grow deep inside me,
so by the time we're finished eating
and packed up in the car
and on our way back to Aunt Bee's,
I can see Gran's love in the food
she's made over the years,
and I can see Granddad's love
in the words he hardly ever speaks,
unless he knows they're needed,
and I can see Mama's love
in leaving us with Aunt Bee,
who loves us in a thousand
fire ways.

One time, back when me and Josh
were still friends,
we put this action figure on the hood
of his mama's car to see
how far down the road to school we'd get
before the figure man fell over.
He held on the entire trip,
flying on his back.

I feel like him today,
flying on my back,
staring at a black sky,
watching Mama's star.

AFRAID

School starts soon, and Aunt Bee
needs to go to her office
to take care of a few things, she says,
so today we're going with her.

My heart beats against my chest
as soon as I shut the car door,
even though I try to tell myself
this isn't the first day of school.
My heart doesn't care, I reckon,
seeing as by the time Aunt Bee
parks the car on a road
down the way from the school,
I'm sweating like I've
walked all the way
from her house to here.

We'll park here, Aunt Bee says.
If someone sees my car,
we'll be here all day.
Aunt Bee winks at us.
Teachers like to talk,
and everybody needs something
from the principal.

A long sidewalk stands in front of us,
ending at a building bigger
than my last school but still
small enough to feel okay.
The grass is impossibly green
for summer. A playground
sits off to the side.

I see all this from the window.
I haven't gotten out yet.
Aunt Bee and Charlie are both
looking at me through the glass.

Nothing to be afraid of,
Aunt Bee says, patting
my shoulder when I
finally open my door
and climb out.

I don't answer, since she can
probably feel the heat through my sleeve.
She doesn't say anything else.
She heads toward the doors,
and we follow.

TOUR

The building is cool and dark.
We follow Aunt Bee into her office,
where important-looking papers
stack her desk much neater than
they stack the corners at home,
and posters with things like
READ TO SUCCEED and
NEVER GIVE UP and
STAY CURIOUS ABOUT THE WORLD
fill her walls.

Me and Charlie sit in seats
that stick to our legs while
Aunt Bee opens one of her drawers
and pulls out a pen and
disappears into a room off
the side of her office.
She comes back with
a bundle of papers.

It only takes her a few minutes,
and then she says, *Let me show
you around, Paulie,* like it's the
most normal thing in the world
to come to a school

in the middle of summer
and walk down empty hallways.
She turns down what she calls
the fifth-grade hall and tells me
about the teachers, three of them,
who are some of the best teachers
in the whole state.

I touch their nameplates,
hanging on the walls
beside the doors,
on my way past.

Aunt Bee shows us the cafeteria,
which will probably be my favorite place,
and then she shows me the music room,
and I think maybe that will be my
favorite place, and then
she stops at the door
of the art room, which will
most definitely be my
favorite place of all.

TEACHER

It surprises me
that someone's inside.

Mr. Langley, Aunt Bee says.

A tall man turns around.
His eyes shine
from all those feet away,
glowing like flashlights.
His skin is dark brown,
and I think that's what
surprises me most.
We didn't have any teachers
like him at my school last year.
No students, either.

When I asked Mama why
the two black boys
who lived on our dirt road
didn't go to my school,
she said they were supposed to,
but people were up in arms
about it and had kept
them out so far.

I don't understand why people
wouldn't let a boy go to a school
on account of his skin color.

Mrs. Adams, Mr. Langley says.
*I didn't think I'd see you
until school started.*

*I brought my nephew
I told you about,* Aunt Bee says,
pushing me forward.
This is Paulie Sanders.
She chokes on the name,
same as my daddy's.

Mr. Langley holds out a hand,
big and thick, with dark fingers
stained by paint.
I shake it, and his grip is
strong and gentle
all at the same time.

*Mr. Langley will be your
art teacher,* Aunt Bee says,
and Mr. Langley
winks at me.

I've heard you like
to draw, he says.

I nod, not sure I could
say anything even if
I wanted to.

Mr. Langley leans close.
He smells sweet like oranges.
Will you show me?
He turns without waiting
for an answer, and I follow him
to the corner he came from.

ECHO

I sketch the big tree in front of
Aunt Bee's house, and Mr. Langley
tells me about the charcoals
he did as a kid, mostly
horses and birds and
his family dog, and then he
shows me what he does now,
flipping through face after face
of people I don't know.
He stops on one that looks
exactly like Aunt Bee.

You know this one, he says.

I look toward the door,
but Aunt Bee and Charlie
have left me. The way
Mr. Langley looks at me,
with those lines crinkling
all around his eyes,
I feel like I've been let in
on some great secret.

And I don't know what
comes over me, but I say,
I want to learn to paint

like Aunt Bee, and then
Mr. Langley is staring at me
like I've said something wrong,
and I wish I could take it back.

She paints? he says.
He sits back in his chair
and closes his sketchbook,
my drawing somewhere
in its middle.
Well, he says.
*I should get you back
to your aunt. I'll walk you.*

And he does, all the way
down one hall after another,
but he stops right before
the front office door and
shakes my hand again
and says, *I'm looking forward
to seeing your work again, Paulie.*
His eyes stare sadness into mine,
and I feel it all the way down
to my toes.
Then he turns away.

His steps echo
a song I don't
understand.

GONE

I forget all about Mr. Langley
and the sad song his feet played,
being as Milo is gone
when we get back home.

I look in every corner,
behind the trees,
in the trees, even though
I know he can't climb them.
I look under a pot that was
turned over in last night's wind,
even though he's too big
to fit under it. I look
through the fence spaces,
into the neighbors' yards,
even though he always
stayed where he was
supposed to.

But Milo
is gone.

SEARCH

I run.
Out the door,
over the front
porch steps,
down the street.

Aunt Bee chases me,
calling my name,
and I hear Charlie's
voice mixed with hers,
but I run and run and run
and don't stop.
I guess they finally understand
what's tearing from my mouth,
since they start yelling
Milo's name, too.

And then we get to the end of that street,
where the yellow lines of a
busier road stop me.
Milo hasn't come running to me
with his tongue hanging out,
like he would if he could hear me,
and the sorrow of it sits me right down
in the middle of the road.

Drops from the sky
pelt my arms and
curled-up legs.

I don't want to go home
without Milo.

Just before Aunt Bee and
Charlie catch up and I'm pulled
from the heated blacktop into
the warm grass and
Aunt Bee's arms,
I think about
how nothing good ever
happens in the rain.

Aunt Bee and Charlie
drag me back home.
I don't even fight them.

WALK

All afternoon and the next day
and the two days after that
I walk the streets, calling
Milo's name loud enough
for everyone to hear, so all
the people come out onto
their porches, asking what
kind of dog it is
I'm looking for.

I miss my
mowing day.

I miss weeding
the flower beds
with Gran.

And I don't care.

CARE

Tonight Aunt Bee calls me home for supper,
her voice ringing out through the streets
from where she stands on the porch,
wearing those eyes that have only
said sorry since Milo disappeared.
I can't look at them anymore.
It hurts too bad,
knowing what
they mean.

We sit around the table,
where Aunt Bee has put
a steaming pot of spaghetti,
but I can't eat, seeing as
my stomach feels like it's
all tied up in great big knots.

I put in a call to the local shelter,
in case he was picked up,
Aunt Bee says to no one
in particular.

Charlie scoots her chair
closer to mine and reaches
to squeeze my hand.

Even though my daddy
brought Milo home for all of us,
he belonged to me.
Everyone knew it, even my daddy.

That's how come he always
told me to take good care of Milo
while he was away at work.

I didn't take care of him
like my daddy wanted me to
after all.

SPEAK

We're clearing away the supper
that no one really ate when the
doorbell rings. Aunt Bee is
the only one who moves,
at least until we hear her cry,
and then me and Charlie are
fighting each other
to get to the door first.

There, standing behind a screen,
is a tall man, dark where
my daddy was light.

In his arms is a form
that looks like it might have
once been a dog.
A black dog,
streaked with red.
A smiling dog
with a twisted neck.
A quiet dog,
no longer breathing.

Milo.

A screech fills the room,
long and loud and terrifying,
like the wail of a
broken animal.

It's only when Charlie
claps her hands over my mouth,
her eyes spilling water all
down her face, and I stumble
back onto the couch, that I
realize it was me who screamed, not the
lump in the stranger's arms.

That animal, the dog, my dog,
couldn't speak like that in the first place.
But he spoke with
his eyes and his smile
and his long pink tongue.

Now he'll never
speak again.

BURY

Aunt Bee takes us home
to bury Milo.

We put his bed, the one she
bought for him to use
in the backyard, in her car.
Aunt Bee carries him out to the car
like a baby, his black head twisting
right out of her arms so it hangs
down to the side.
His eyes are closed.

I sit with him in the back,
even though it's my turn
to ride in the front. Charlie
sits in the back, too.

No one says a word
all the way home.

GRAVE

I'm the first one in the house.
It doesn't look all that different
with Mama gone, except that
her bed is made up.
Mama never used to
make up her bed, being as
she was just going to
sleep in it that night.
My daddy, though, he wanted
all our beds made every single day,
before we even came to breakfast,
back when we used to eat together.
Mama used to say that was
the army man talking.

Aunt Bee carries Milo and his bed
toward the woods while I
watch from Mama's window.
Then I follow, so I can pick
the spot where he'll be buried.
I want to bury him on the edge
of the woods and our backyard,
since he loved the woods
as much as he loved our yard.

Charlie and Aunt Bee dig a hole,
right where I've pointed,
and when they're done,
I pick him up, without his bed.
I know he'd want the feel
of the dirt under him
instead of a pillow.
I lay him in the hole.

We don't talk. We just stare,
and then, when the sad starts
hurting my throat, I shove
some dirt into the hole
with my toe so Aunt Bee
and Charlie know I'm ready
for them to cover my dog forever.

The dirt sticks to his fur
and collects around his mouth
and wraps around his tail.
And then his whole body
disappears.

I arrange some leaves and sticks
on top of the dirt piled over his hole.

Charlie hands me a cross
I didn't see her carry here,
and all over it are little scenes
of me and Milo, painted to look
just like pictures.

I look at Aunt Bee.
She nods.

I swallow all the tears
sitting in my throat,
and I jam the cross
into the ground,
marking the place
where my best friend rests.

WORN

After we've had a few
minutes of quiet looking,
me and Charlie and Aunt Bee
go back inside, where they
unpack the lunch they brought
and I stand beside the window,
watching the front porch
where Milo used to lay,
on those days the sun stripes
would turn him zebra.

The porch is cracked and worn
where his tail thumped the wood.

I turn away and
walk into the kitchen,
back to what's left of my own
cracked and worn world.

CAKE

A lemon cake, yellow on the outside
hiding yellow in the middle,
sits on Gran's table.

It's amazing to me, every time,
that Gran remembers everyone's
favorite cake, without even asking.
She used to make carrot cake
for my daddy and chocolate
for my mama.

I've tried all day not to
think about Mama, being as
she should be back by now.
I don't want to spoil
my special day with questions.

Mama always used my birthday
to celebrate the end of summer
and the beginning of the school year.
I guess Aunt Bee liked that idea,
since we're all gathered
at Gran's house today.

PARTY

Last time I had a birthday party
my daddy came, and he stood
right in the middle of everyone,
singing just as loud as he could.
I sure wish everything didn't
remind me of him.

I reckon everybody notices
I'm not feeling too excited
about my special day,
since Aunt Bee squeezes
my shoulder real hard
and Gran lights those eleven candles
spread out on the top of the cake
and Granddad pulls on his guitar
and they all start singing
the happiest version
of "Happy Birthday"
I've ever heard
in my whole life.

Something about it
warms me from
the inside.

Gran cuts pieces of cake
while Charlie piles presents
in front of me. Some new shoes
from Gran and Granddad.
Paint supplies from Aunt Bee.

Charlie's gift is a rectangle,
flat and heavy and hard.

I tear into the plain blue paper.
Inside is a frame with a
thousand buttons glued
to a piece of the fabric.

The way the buttons
curve together makes it look
just like the road that
took my daddy.

And I don't think she
expected it at all, but I cry,
and I can't stop.

I can't stop.
I don't really know why.

It's just that those buttons,
on their insides, hold all
the colors of us.
Orange for Charlie.
Green for me.
Yellow for Mama.
Blue for my daddy.
All our favorites wrapped
around each other.

We are still together,
even in our worlds apart.
I don't know if this is
what Charlie meant
when she made it for me,
but it's what I see.

FALL 1972

FIRST

We leave before
the sun has fully come up.

Aunt Bee talks the whole way
about how this year
is going to be different.
Our schools have been slow
to desegregate, she says.
But the government
cracked down this year.
About time, too, is what I say.

She says she's expecting
protestors, so we'll have to
be careful on our way in.

On a street that leads up
near the elementary school,
we pass a whole group of people
carrying signs and yelling.
They don't move off the road,
so Aunt Bee drives real slow,
winding around them
like she's done this
sort of thing before.

They hit our car as we drive past.
Every smack is so loud
it makes me jump.
The signs say things like
STOP THE RACE MIXING and
RACE MIXING IS COMMUNISM and
GO BACK TO AFRICA, LANGLEY & KIDS.

Oh, for God's sake,
Aunt Bee says.
She says a few more words
I'm not supposed to repeat.
Charlie looks back at me
with big eyes.

And then we're past them
and pulling into the
school parking lot and the
sun is staring at us,
like it's determined
today will be a good day.

PROTEST

Aunt Bee walks Charlie
to the place where her bus
will drop off and pick up,
and I follow them.

We try not to notice
the line of boys and girls
and parents out front holding signs
that say things like,
WE WON'T GO TO SCHOOL WITH NEGROES and
STRIKE AGAINST INTEGRATION and
WESTHEIMER SCHOOL DISTRICT IS COMING.

I don't know what all
the fuss is about. It's just
a different color skin.

It'll be worse at your
school, Charlotte,
Aunt Bee says.

A girl waiting in line, with skin
the color of Granddad's coffee,
looks up at Aunt Bee's words.

She catches Charlie's eye
and then looks away.

Have a good day,
Aunt Bee says, and she gives
Charlie a quick hug.

Charlie smiles, but it's easy
to see it's not a real one.
It shakes at the edges.

We turn away,
and I hear Charlie say,
I'm Charlie, and the
other girl says,
I'm Harriet, and I can't help
but think my sister is the
bravest girl I know.

MEET

Aunt Bee is some kind of celebrity,
or at least it seems that way,
since everybody in the hall
knows her. At least the light-skinned kids do.
The dark-skinned kids stare and
don't say anything.
I try to meet the eyes
of some of them,
but they just look away,
like they're ashamed to be here.

The first thing
Aunt Bee does every time
someone waves or gives her a hug
or opens their mouth at all
is push me forward and say,
This is my nephew, Paulie Sanders,
like she wants everyone
in the world to know me, too.

It must take us an hour
to get back to Aunt Bee's office.

*I'll walk you to your class
in a few minutes, Paulie,* she says.

My stomach jumps, over and over,
like something is stuck inside it,
even though I only ate half the fried egg
Aunt Bee cooked me this morning.

I take out my sketchbook,
since drawing always
calms me.

CLASS

I'm halfway through
a picture of Aunt Bee
at her desk when she says,
All right. You ready?

No. I'm not at all ready.
But I close the pad
and stuff it back in my bag.

We walk down the hallway
until we reach a door
that says MRS. MARTELL.

The first thing I notice
inside the room
is that the light-skinned kids
sit up front
and the dark-skinned kids
huddle in the back.

At the front of the room
is a woman who looks
much younger than Mama,
with dark red hair
and eyes the color of fog.

This is Paulie, Aunt Bee says,
and some of the kids
turn and look at me.
Mrs. Martell surprises me
with a hug. She smells
like lemon soap.

Welcome to our class, Paulie.
She smiles with big
pearly white teeth.

I wonder how much
Aunt Bee has told her about me,
and if that's why
she's being so nice.

Aunt Bee hugs me real quick,
like she did with Charlie,
and then she's gone.

I've never felt so alone
in my life, even though
there are people all
around me.

The first bell rings,
and I sit in the back,
even though I have light skin,
not dark skin,
and try not to meet
a single person's eye.

IMPOSSIBLE

The lunchroom is
just like my classroom:
light-skinned kids separated
from dark-skinned kids.

I don't sit with anyone
at lunch. I don't walk
with anyone back to class.

And then the bell rings
and the day is over,
and I'm pushing through
a crowded hallway, where some
white kids are hissing
mean things to black kids,
who walk with their heads down.
I'm trying to get to
Aunt Bee's office, but I can't
remember where it is.
Everyone's sure of where
they're going except me.

So I just
keep walking.

HANDS

A noise at the end of the hallway
makes me turn.

Who's there? I say,
my heart thumping.

Greg, a voice says.
It's high and shrill,
like maybe I've scared
whoever owns it, too.

When he steps into the light
I see a boy, smaller than me,
with eyes and skin so dark
they make the whites of his eyes glow.
He pushes dark, curly hair
from his forehead,
and sweat makes it
stand straight up.
Students aren't allowed
back here, he says.
What are you doing?

I guess I could
ask him the same.

Nothing, I say.
My voice is hard.
This boy's done
nothing wrong but scare me.

He leans closer.
Are you crying? he says.

Then all my rage
comes out into my hands,
and before I can stop it, before
I even know what's happening,
he's on his back and
I'm running down one hallway
after another.

BULLY

Somehow I find myself
in front of Aunt Bee's office door.
I stand outside, trying to
catch my breath.

Aunt Bee is packing up to go.
Charlie sits in the chair
where I sat drawing Aunt Bee
at her desk this morning.
She looks at me
and back down at her book,
like maybe she doesn't want me
to read her eyes.

Paulie, Aunt Bee says.
I was starting to worry.
Where were you?

I shrug.
Exploring, I say.
I look at my hands,
the ones that
pushed a boy down.

Now I'm
my daddy,
the bully.

I know I don't
have to be.

It's just that when I
pushed that boy down
it felt like I had some control
over the hurricane of feelings,
whipping inside me.
I didn't have to be sad
or mad or confused
or scared or hopeless.
I didn't have to be
the boy who lost his daddy
because of a black man.

We follow Aunt Bee
out to the car.
It's hot inside and
real hard to breathe.

BENT

I guess Aunt Bee knows
me and Charlie don't really
want to talk about our days,
since she doesn't ask us
any questions.
She turns on the radio instead.

It's reporting about all the fights
that broke out in school hallways today,
and the determination of white parents
to start their own segregated school district,
about the *spirit of protest*
that has taken Houston by storm
ever since black students
at a local university
pelted police officers
with bottles and rocks
for forcefully breaking up
a student demonstration
in Emancipation Park.

My God, Aunt Bee says.
The whole world's
lost its marbles.

I listen and watch the green fields
outside the window. That's when
I see something I didn't notice
this morning when the world
was still mostly dark.

In the middle of a field
there is a tree, tall and wide and full;
the wind is twisting its branches
and tearing its leaves and
bending it near in two,
and the tree can't do
anything about it.
It just moves where
the wind takes it.

We are all like that tree, I think.
Bent near in two
by the world.

NEXT

A whole week of school
and it's more of the same.
Sit alone. Walk alone.
Don't speak.
I hate this place.

I see the boy I pushed down
twice every day, at lunch
and in the hallway, going
back to class. He must be
a fifth grader, too, just a
really small one, seeing as
we have the same lunch period.
He carries his food in a brown bag
and sits at a table
with boys and girls
who look like him.

He's always watching me.
He's either scared or curious.
I don't know which it is,
since I can't ever find the
nerve to look in his eyes.
It's not for the reasons
you might think, either.

Something must be wrong with me.
Charlie would say I'm
being dramatic.
But I don't feel bad for what I did,
pushing him down. I feel
like I could do it again.

And what makes it worse
is that he is one of the kids
the people protesting out front
say shouldn't be here.
Do I believe them, deep down?
I didn't think I did,
but what about my actions?

I'm afraid of what comes next.

DESK

Mr. Langley remembers me when
I walk through the door,
but he only talks for a minute.
There are other kids coming in, too,
and they all want to talk to him.

Small easels sit on all the desks
in the room, along with
watercolor rectangles, a cup of water,
and four paintbrushes.
Paper is clipped onto the easels.
I walk to a desk
in the back corner.

It's not until class has started
and Mr. Langley holds up a
vase of flowers and says
we need to paint what we see
that I notice who is closest
to me. It's Greg, the boy
I pushed down.

PAINT

I try to focus on my painting,
but it's hard. Greg keeps
looking over and
whispering, *Wow,*
loud enough for me
to hear it.

I steal a few glances
at his painting,
but it's not good.
Not even a little bit.

I paint different colors
than the ones on the vase
Mr. Langley put on his desk.
Blues and blacks and reds
that don't look as dark as
I'd like them to, since
we're using watercolors.

When Mr. Langley walks by,
he stops and stares. *Interesting
color choice, Paulie,* he says
before he moves away.

I keep dipping and swirling
until the bell rings,
until most of the kids
leave the room, until it's just
me and Greg and Mr. Langley.

MOTHER

Greg puts his brushes and watercolors away
before I do and walks toward
Mr. Langley. He points behind him.
He's really good, he says.

Mr. Langley nods.
I know, he says.

A hot wind climbs up my neck.
These are nice words
from a boy I hurt, and they burn.
I don't deserve them.

How are you holding up?
Mr. Langley says.

Greg shrugs.
*The signs out front
are ugly,* he says.

It'll die down, Mr. Langley says.
*Eventually they'll get
used to integration.*
He clears his throat and
tilts his head. *No one's*

hurt you, have they?
That's what I'm concerned
about—the violence.

I hold my breath,
but Greg shakes his head.
They mostly act like
I'm not even here.

Well. Mr. Langley puts a hand
on Greg's shoulder and walks him
toward the door.
He says something real quiet,
like maybe he doesn't
want me to hear.
At the door, he says,
How's your mother?

I don't even hear Greg's answer,
being as my blood starts shouting
in my ears. My hands clench,
and I have to concentrate real hard
to keep them from ripping
the paper in front of me.

Why do some get to have mothers
and others don't?

FRIEND

Paulie. I jump.
Mr. Langley is right
beside me, pointing
at the flowers on my paper.
Why did you change
them? he says.

I look at the picture.
I guess I wasn't paying attention.
Instead of the lilies
Mr. Langley has in his vase,
I painted tulips.

Mama's favorite.

I shrug and look away.
I can feel Mr. Langley's
eyes on me, like he knows
why I did it and he didn't really
need to ask me
at all.

But how could
he know?

Would you like to help me
with something after school? he says.
He waves his hand at some
crates beside me. In them
are cans of spray paint
in all different colors.

What is it? I say.
It's the first time I've spoken
in a class since the
school year began.

You'll see, he says,
smiling so the skin around his eyes
wrinkles like crumpled paper.

Okay, I say.
I'll just have to let
Aunt Bee know.

Come as soon as the
bell rings, he says,
like he already knows
what Aunt Bee will say.

I walk down the hall,
counting the hours
until the school day ends.

BUILDING

When the bell finally rings
and Aunt Bee waves me
out her office door, I meet Mr. Langley
outside the art room.
He's holding the crate
of spray paint.

Follow me, he says.

He takes me to a building
behind the school,
an old one that might have
once been red, but I can't
tell for sure.
It's mostly brown now.

Mr. Langley walks around
to the side that faces the street.
The sun is hot and bright.

We'll paint the whole thing, he says.
But we'll save this side for last.

Today? I say, being as it's a
really big building for
painting in a day.

Mr. Langley laughs.
It's a nice laugh, not too loud,
one that comes from down
deep in his belly. *No, he says.*
It will take us lots of days.
We're supposed to paint
a mural on each side.

I wonder why he wants me
to help him with something
like this. Something that will
be here forever. Something
the whole school will see.

Why? I say, but it must not
come out quite right,
since he doesn't
give me the whole
answer I want.

Your aunt wants to make
this building pretty again, he says.
It used to be. And then . . .
His face turns darker
and real sad. He turns away,

like whatever's inside isn't
something he ever
wants to see again.

GOOD

What's in there? I say.

He looks at me for a long time.
Maintenance supplies, he says.
He walks to the back
of the building, where we
left the crate. *We'll paint
the front and back together,*
he says. *But I thought we could
each take a side and
see what happens.*

Why me? I say.

Mr. Langley picks up a purple can
and a blue can from the crate.
*Because Greg thinks
you're good,* he says.
He grins. *And so do I.*

I'm so shocked I don't find
more words before Mr. Langley says,
Pick your colors, and then
disappears to his own side.

START

I stand there staring at the colors
for such a long time, not knowing
what to choose, that Mr. Langley
pokes his head out again.
Need help? he says.

I just don't know what to do, I say.
I don't know where to start.

Mr. Langley walks back to the paints,
puts his down into the missing slots.
He squeezes my shoulder.
Sometimes the hardest place
is the starting line, he says.

I think he might be
talking about more
than just the painting.
It's the way he's looking at me,
like he knows all the questions
I've asked myself since my
daddy left and my mama ran off.

I follow him back to his side,
to see what he's doing.

A big YOU stands blue
against the brown, and
right beside it, CAN is
written in purple.
He holds the new spray can
up for a minute, and then he
paints over the words
with orange.

I walk back to my side,
stopping to pick up the green.
I paint what my hands want,
and even though I've never
done this with a can of spray paint,
something starts to take shape
in front of me. I only get half
the green grass done before
it's time to go.

But I know I can start now,
seeing as how I already have.

I help Mr. Langley carry the paint
back to his classroom, even though
he doesn't really need my help.

We walk down
the hall together, toward
Aunt Bee.

TRUTH

Aunt Bee sends me
into her office, where
Charlie is waiting.
She says she needs to talk
with Mr. Langley in private.

Me and Charlie hear them
talking in their low voices,
and we don't even have to
look at each other to know
it's time to sit still and listen.

You didn't tell him,
Aunt Bee says.

No, Mr. Langley says.

I don't want him to know.
Not yet, Aunt Bee says.
We'll give it some time.

I know, Mr. Langley says.

For a second, I think
they're talking about Mama,

and I feel anger blowing
like a hot breath across my face.
Then Aunt Bee says, *He's got*
enough to burden his mind
without knowing the truth
about that building, and I feel
like someone knocked me
clean off my feet.

CRY

They're quiet for a minute
before Mr. Langley says,
Paulie says you paint?

My heart beats hard
against my chest. I didn't know
I wasn't supposed to tell.
I want to yell the words to Aunt Bee
before she can get mad at me.

Aunt Bee doesn't answer
before Mr. Langley says,
*I don't know why you
couldn't tell me,* and
something about his voice—
the way it holds all the
disappointment and hurt
and sadness in the world—
makes me and Charlie
look at each other.
Her eyes are wide.
After all— he starts to say,
but Aunt Bee interrupts him.

I don't paint anymore, she says.
Her voice is weak, like
something is stuck in her throat.

She isn't telling the truth.
Me and Charlie always sneak
in her room when she's
gone to the post office.
Those canvas stacks get bigger,
mostly pictures of Mama
and Granddad and
especially my daddy.

They don't say anything for so long
that me and Charlie get up and
look out the door Aunt Bee
forgot to close behind her.

Mr. Langley is still there,
and his arms wrap all the way
around Aunt Bee. She's shaking.

I could count on one hand
how many times I've seen
Aunt Bee cry.

1. The night those lights
shone red and blue
through the rain.

2. The day she stood up
to talk at my daddy's funeral
and she choked on
the word *brother*.

3. Today.

KNOWING

When I can finally move,
I walk back to my chair.
I have so many questions
I don't even know where to start.
Charlie whispers, *He loves her.*
And she loves him.

It's something I never thought about,
but I see now how it explains everything.
That day I told him she could paint,
and he left without talking to her,
like it changed something for him.
The way her eyes watched him
the day she introduced us.
The ghost in his voice today.

I don't know if I like
knowing this, though,
since knowing just adds
more questions.

WEB

On the way in to school this morning,
I stopped to watch a spider in the grass,
held up by a web, where a thousand
drops of dew made the whole thing
look like a piece of Bubble Wrap
my daddy used to pop with me.

This morning I thought
it was something pretty enough
to stop and see, but now I know
it was a picture of me.

I am a spider stuck in a web,
surrounded by dewdrop questions.
Every move I make
sends answers I don't like
splashing deep enough
to drown me.

FORGIVENESS

Mr. Langley told me we'd only
be painting on Mondays,
so I have to find something else to do
every other day of the week.
I don't like waiting for Charlie
to get off the school bus
or sitting in Aunt Bee's office,
so I've taken to exploring the streets
around the school.

I don't tell Aunt Bee.
She doesn't do things
like Mama did them.

Daddy told me once
it's better to ask for
forgiveness than permission.

STREET

The roads are always quiet,
since not too many students
live in these houses near the school.
Most of the people I pass are old,
walking their dogs
in the same bent-over way.
They smile at me and say hello,
even though I don't know them.
I always stop to pet their dogs.

I don't usually turn on
any other streets, but today
I take only one right and one left,
so I'll remember the
way back.

The houses down this street
are chipped and crumbling.
They look like my old house.

A kid shouts from
somewhere up ahead,
so I follow the sound.
When I get closer, I see
it's Greg, bouncing a ball

up and down, shouting like
he's some kind of sports
announcer or something.

A woman sits on the porch,
watching him. I'm not too close
to them, but even from here
I can see her skin,
darker than Greg's,
and her wheelchair.

WATCH

I duck behind a bush.
I don't know why.
I just want to
watch, I guess.

Greg keeps right on playing
and shouting and chasing the ball.
When he misses the hoop,
he races toward the porch,
bouncing his ball
so it thumps on the wood.

The hollow of the bounce
is like the hollowing of me.
He calls her the name
I don't use anymore.

Want something to
drink, Mama? he says.

I'll take some ice water.
Thank you, baby, she says,
in a voice I can barely hear.
She holds her hand out
to touch his face as he passes.

The screen door slams
behind him, and I turn to go.

PAIN

I can't put to rights
what I've just seen,
a mama in a wheelchair,
a boy getting her water.
There's too much shouting
in my head.

The trees blow me
down the road I came,
gusting hard like
my anger.

Why am I mad?

I guess it's because
a broken mama is
better than a gone one.

The brick school building
shows up quicker than I expect
and when I see it,
I can't stop myself.
I kick a wall.

My toes scream their pain
all the way to Aunt Bee's office,
but it's nothing like the
pain in my heart.

LONELY

Charlie's in her room,
working on some school project;
I'm sitting in the living room alone,
reading Aunt Bee's favorite
Agatha Christie book.

Aunt Bee sits down beside me.
She doesn't turn on the television.
She just stares at the blank screen.

I try to keep reading, but it's hard.
I'm waiting for her to say something.
I know that's what she wants to do,
but for some reason she doesn't.

Are you liking school, Paulie?
she finally says. She turns
to look at me. She doesn't
seem to notice I'm reading her
favorite book again, even though
I've already read it three times.
It's one of my favorites now, too.

Before I can answer,
she says, *Do you like it here?*

I think of Mrs. Martell
reading to us
from the front of the room,
how it warms me all through
because it reminds me
of life before my daddy left,
when Mama would read
to me and Charlie
from the books she loved as a kid.
I think of Mr. Langley and his
art room, how every corner of it
feels like home. And then
I think of my lonely lunch table
and the lonely halls and the
lonely minutes before school.

SAFE

I guess I wait too long to answer,
because Aunt Bee says,
I just want to know that
we made the right decision.
She turns a mug around and around
on the table beside the couch,
like she needs something
to do with her hands.

What would she do if I said
I didn't like school?
Would she send me back
to my old one, where
Josh and Brian would ignore me
in the halls?

The thought of that makes me say,
I like it all right.
I look her straight in the eye
so she'll believe me,
since I don't want to go back
to a school where every kid
knows what my daddy did.

Aunt Bee lets out a long breath.
Okay, she says. *Okay.*
I just wanted to make sure.

She takes a sip from her cup
and then sets it back down.
She looks at me again.
I try not to look away.
It's not easy to make friends
in a new place, she says.
She touches my hair.
It's not easy to trust people with your heart,
after all you've been through.

I wonder, how does
Aunt Bee know
exactly how I feel?

But sometimes we have to try, Aunt Bee says,
and I don't know if she's still talking
about me anymore.
Sometimes we have to risk
the heartbreak
because we're tired
of trying to live life alone.

I watch Aunt Bee for a while,
and it's not until she takes
another drink from her cup
that her eyes come back to me.

Anyhow, she says,
and there's nothing else.

She turns on the television,
to some station that reports news
all hours of the day,
but I'm not interested in seeing
more protests or hearing about
a new school district
or kids who'll be voting this election year
on account of the voting age changing,
so I go back to reading my book.
Except I'm not really reading,
since the words in my brain
are running into the words
on the page.

I think Aunt Bee is wrong.

It's not that bad
living life alone.

The opposite of friends
isn't lonely.
The opposite of friends
is safe.

EASY

It's really easy
to do it.

I just don't think.
I stick out my foot
and he trips so his lunch
falls right out of his
hands and into mine.
I don't think when I take off
running and pull out the
peanut butter sandwich
and the bag of sliced cucumbers
and the red apple and scatter them
behind me like a trail leading straight
into the lunchroom.
I don't think when I read the note
from his mama in a wheelchair
and let it fly out of my fingers
like I fly out the cafeteria doors,
toward the wooden bench where I sit,
alone, and eat the lunch
I packed myself.

I don't think about why
or what could happen
or what it means.

It's easy.

RUN

I don't even get in trouble
for what I've done.
At first I think maybe
Greg didn't see who it was,
but then today, when I pass
him in the hallway,
he looks me straight in the eyes,
and I can tell he knows.

He doesn't look angry or scared.
Just sad.
And that gets caught in my throat.
So I stick my foot out again,
and I only hear
the slap of his hands against
the floor.

I run away as fast as I can,
ducking into a bathroom.

I hate him. I hate him so much.
And I don't know why.

NOTE

Someone else would probably have
laughed, but I don't feel like laughing,
so I let myself cry for a while.

When I finally get back to class,
a note is waiting on
Mrs. Martell's desk.

Please send Paulie
to the office, it says.
Mrs. Martell has kind eyes
when she tells me to
pack my things, since
the bell will probably ring
while I'm gone.

The words fall
like weights clamped
around my feet.

HALLWAY

The hallway to the office is long.
I don't want to see her face.
I don't want to hear her voice.
I don't want to feel her disappointment.

What will she say about
what I've done?

I know what Mama
would say: *Don't be
like your daddy.*

And I know what I
would yell back, right
into the cheeks and chin
and eyes she gave me:
I'm trying.

If someone could just
show me how.

SCREAMING

I walk through the office doors.
Aunt Bee's assistant, Mrs. Blake,
waves me on through.
She's waiting for you, she says,
and I try not to cry.

Aunt Bee is sitting at her desk
when I step into her office.
I sit down in the seat I
always sit in, like it will
somehow keep me safe
from what's coming.

She stares at my face
for a minute before she says,
Is something wrong, Paulie?
She sounds concerned,
not a bit angry like
I thought she'd be.

I shrug
and look at my feet.

She clears her throat.
*I wanted to give you a little time
to adjust to school,* she says.

But now that you have, I think
you're ready. I watch her stand.
I'm so confused my face
starts burning.

Does she know
or doesn't she?

Aunt Bee kneels in front of me.
She takes one of my hands in hers.
I want you to meet the school
counselor today, she says.
You'll be seeing her for a while,
just to talk.

I don't hear anything else she says
after that. The whole room fades
and the only person I see
is my daddy.

BROKEN

Mama asked my daddy to
go to counseling once,
just like Aunt Bee is asking me to do,
and he exploded into a wild rage.
There's nothing wrong with me, he yelled,
over and over again until I wondered
if maybe there was.
He added other words
after a while. *I don't need no doctors
telling me there is,* he said.
I'm not weak.
I'm not damaged.

And then he threw the glass in his hand
and followed the throw with a fist
to Mama's jaw. His hand went through
the top screen of the door
on his way out.

Me and Charlie stood
in the middle of a room
where a glass had broken
in a corner and our mama
sat broken on the floor.

WRONG

I try to find words,
but the only ones
turning through my head are,
There's nothing wrong with me.
There's nothing wrong with me.
There's nothing wrong with me.

But what if
there is?

Sometimes it just helps to talk
to someone, Aunt Bee says.
She's dropped my hand.
God knows I'm not so great
at that part.

No. I can't talk to some stranger,
not about me or my daddy or
Mama or Charlie. I can't talk
about all those memories
that belong to us.

I won't share our secrets.
I won't betray
my daddy like that.

I don't know how to explain it
to Aunt Bee, though, so I just run.
I run until the whole world blurs
and I don't know where I am
or where I'm going, and I don't care
if I never find my way
back again.

RIPPLES

I find a little pool of water
down past all the houses.
The water is clear enough
to see through. I watch my feet
and the ripples that shake
around them when I move.
They're like the ripples that
shake around my life.

I wish my life
would stop rippling.

I stand in the water and think
about my daddy's hands.
I think about all those times
he didn't come home and
Gran or Aunt Bee had to come
stay with us while Mama
went out looking.
I think of a drawer beside their bed
where I thought scissors might be,
but instead I found piles of pills
spilled out inside.

I think of the dead man and
those men who shot my daddy
and Josh and Brian and the words
kids flung down the hallways
in the days before Mama
pulled me and Charlie out.

I can't tell a counselor all that.

I guess I'll just have to learn
how to hide my secrets like
Aunt Bee hides hers.

BACK

My whole body feels hot
after my run and all this thinking,
but the water feels cool and soft
and right, like a mama's touch
or a daddy's hug. So I close my eyes
and I let it love me like
I guess they never could.

And when my heart feels
even and smooth, like the
surface of the water,
I walk barefoot back
to the school, surprised
I know the way.

HELP

Mrs. Walsh is short and young,
more like a student than a grown-up.

She pulled me out of
writing my spelling words
three times on a page, so I
didn't mind much at the time,
but now I'm here, and her eyes
are like the prettiest water I've
ever seen. I think they can
see right through me.

She asks me some questions,
how I like the school,
what I think of my classes,
which subject is my favorite.

And I start thinking this
might be easy, since I'm
watching the clock, and it's
ticking toward the end of
thirty minutes. These questions
I can answer.

But then Mrs. Walsh says,
It's hard to be a boy without
his parents, isn't it? and I
don't know what to say.

All those times I wished
my mean daddy gone and
a nice one in his place
come pelting me like giant stones.

Mrs. Walsh looks at me,
and I hold on to my chair like
her looking will somehow
sweep me away in those
clear waters.

Then she says, *It's like walking*
down a road with no traffic lights
and the sky is getting darker
and we can only see more headlights
coming at us, blinding us,
and we don't know if
we should cross the street
or just stop altogether.

The whole time she's talking,
she never looks away.

She leans across her desk
and takes my hand.
Her voice is soft when
she says, *I promise, Paulie,
I will help you find
your way across.
But you have to help me.*

And the next thing I know,
I'm nodding and wiping water
from my eyes and it's
time to leave, except I don't
really want to, since this place
feels warm and dry and
safe enough to stand on
my own two feet.

But Aunt Bee is waiting at the door,
so I follow her out, turning back
only once when Mrs. Walsh says,
I'll see you next week, Paulie.

Okay, I say, and I mean it.

FROZEN

Outside the door,
sitting on a bench,
is Greg. He stands
when the door closes
behind me. He stares
at me like he might
say something, but I
look away.

Next week Mrs. Walsh will know
something else about me, I guess.
His visit with her has to be about me,
since Greg couldn't possibly need
Mrs. Walsh to help him find
his way across anything.
He still has a mama, after all.

I guess that place isn't
as safe as I thought.

For some reason,
instead of sad, I just
feel frozen, like maybe
I expected this all along.

Like maybe I knew
a boy like me could
never find safe.

BROTHER

Mr. Langley is painting the wall
on the other side of mine.
He's much further along
than I am, since he's painting a sky
and I'm painting the field
that leads to Gran's pond,
and I can't seem to get
the bluebonnets and
Indian paintbrushes right.

I try and try again,
but nothing looks
the way I see it in my head,
so I walk around to his side
and sit in the grass,
watching him.

He doesn't say anything for a while,
so I think maybe he doesn't know
I'm watching. But then he says,
Finished? and looks back at me.

I shake my head.
He sets down his
can of spray paint and

sits down beside me. We both
stare at his picture of a bright blue
sky and puffy white clouds he's
shaped into animals and
faces and hands.

I'm trying to paint a dragon, he says,
pointing to the cloud in the very
center of the wall. It doesn't look
like a dragon at all.
Can't seem to get it right today.
He smiles at me and
stares back at his picture.

After a few minutes, he says,
Dragons were my brother's favorite.
He folds his legs under him and
leans his elbows into his knees.
*My brother was the greatest man
I ever knew.*

DRAGON

Mr. Langley tells me a story
about two brothers whose daddy
drove away on a motorcycle one day
and never came back.
One brother later lost his bearings
when the world dumped its rain
and the other brother carried
the lost back to life.

He tells me how he spent
those days after his breakdown
searching the sky with his brother
and his brother's boy.

Two men and a little boy
staring at clouds, trying
to find the answers to life,
Mr. Langley says. His eyes
turn real sad.
He saved me.
So now I try to save others.

He doesn't look at me,
but I think he says that
last part for me.

Does your brother live
around here? I say.

Mr. Langley squints up at the sky.
He died last year, he says, and then
he jumps to his feet and
runs back to the building.
He picks up the can he threw down
a while ago and shakes it and
starts spraying.

When he steps back,
away from the center cloud,
it doesn't look like a white
blob anymore. It looks like
a dragon blowing smoke rings.

He is grinning when
he turns around, and
I can't help but join him.

MEAN

I leave Greg alone for a while,
until one day it's just me and him,
standing near the bus stop where
Charlie will be dropped off.
I feel myself turn mean.
I feel myself hate him
for having a mother
or for being black
like the man my daddy died for
or maybe both those things
tangled up together.

He looks surprised when
I walk up close and stare at him
for one second. Two seconds. Three.

And maybe I want to get caught.
Maybe I want someone to help me
know what to do with all this anger.
Maybe that's why I hit him
in the mouth this time.

What? he says, but I hit him again,
and this time he loses his balance
and lands hard on the sidewalk.

I hold him down, but I don't hit him again
until he says, *We could be friends, Paulie,*
and then I don't know
what happens exactly.

I just know that somehow
Charlie is there, pulling me
off him, and that Greg's nose
is puffy and bleeding and that
Charlie's eyes are saying
something I don't want to hear.
Don't be like our daddy, Paulie.

And then I feel a hand
on my shoulder and a
familiar voice say, *Paulie,*
and I can't stay there, with
Charlie and Greg and Mr. Langley
all seeing and knowing just how
messed up I am, so I pull away
and run again.

I run past all the familiar houses
and all the unfamiliar ones, and
I run past Greg's porch,

where his mama waits for him
in her wheelchair and waves and
calls out *Hi there* when I pass,
and I keep on running until all
the houses fall away
and I'm alone.

FOUND

Aunt Bee is the one
who finds me.

I must not have gone
as far as I thought,
being as it doesn't take her long.
She says nothing, just opens the
car door for me, and we drive
in silence back toward the school.

No one's angry, Paulie, she finally says.
Her voice stretches tight in her throat,
like she's trying hard not to cry.
We just want to understand.

I watch the sky out the side window
and imagine all the clouds are animals.
There's a swan and a snail with a
crooked shell and a chicken with hair
and really big tail feathers.

UNDERSTAND

Too soon, we're back at the school
and then we're walking through
the doors and then we're inside
Aunt Bee's office, where everyone
is waiting for us.

Mr. Langley stands.
Charlie and Greg sit in chairs,
but Charlie gets up when
I walk in. Her eyes are
red and puffy.

Aunt Bee wheels her chair around the desk.
Mr. Langley touches her shoulder
before kneeling on the floor
in front of me and Greg.
He looks mostly at Greg, not at me.
I guess I won't be painting
that building with him anymore.
My chest cramps into a knot.

I wish I had my sketchbook.
Then I would have a place
to hide from all their eyes.

What happened?
Aunt Bee says.

I already told you,
Greg says. *Nothing.*

Mr. Langley puts his hand
on Greg's knee. *Let's hear
from Paulie now, Greg,* he says.

I shake my head. I don't understand
why Greg would protect me.
I don't understand how he could
still want to, after what I've done.

I do understand that I have to
tell the truth now.

SORRY

I don't look at anyone
when I say those shameful
words: *I hit him.*

Why? Aunt Bee says.
I can feel their eyes on me,
but I keep staring at my shoes
that don't look so new anymore,
even though they're the newest
I've ever had.

Since I can't answer
Aunt Bee's question,
I say the only words I can.
I don't know. And the sadness
moves all around my words
and into the back of my throat
and down my cheeks. I bend over,
shaking in a chair that's too hard
and an office that's too cold.

Someone's arms wrap me tight.
At first I think it's Aunt Bee,
but she hasn't gotten to me yet.

It's Mr. Langley, and that
makes me cry even harder,
since I thought for sure he'd
give up on me now that I've
bullied a boy I barely know,
a boy with the same skin color as him.
But he's holding me and then
Aunt Bee is there saying, *Oh, Paulie,*
and then everything I've wanted
to say for weeks is spilling out
and all I know is it needs
to be let out.

I'm sorry, I say. *I'm sorry for
destroying your lunch.*
I'm sorry for tripping you.
I'm sorry for hurting you.

I don't know if anyone
can even understand me,
but I have to try.

I don't want to be like my daddy.
I don't. I don't want to
hurt people like he did.

Mr. Langley's arms wrap even tighter,
and it's the only way I know I've said
those terrible words
about my daddy out loud.

BREATHE

Someone touches my back,
and I turn, and it's Greg
standing there, crying, too.
His nose is swollen where
I hit him. How many times
did I hit him? I don't
even remember.

I forgive you, he says,
and maybe that's what
everyone in the room was
waiting on, since we all
breathe one big breath
together.

SKY

Mr. Langley takes Greg's hand
and says, *I'll walk him home,*
and Aunt Bee nods.
Me and Charlie gather our bags
so we can follow Aunt Bee
out to the car.

We pass them on the edge
of the schoolyard. They're sitting
in the grass, pointing toward the sky,
smiling like they've discovered
something great.

And that's when I know.
Greg is the nephew who
helped save Mr. Langley's life.
Greg has a daddy who died, too.

I guess we're not so
different after all.

HOLE

The next day Mr. Langley
takes me out to the building,
even though it's not one of our
days to paint.

We're not going to paint today,
he says, like he knows exactly
what I'm thinking. *We're just
going to sit and look and see.*

I don't really know what this means,
but he sits down in the grass,
so I sit down beside him.
The ground is colder now,
like winter is sneaking closer.
So I pull my knees to my chest
and wrap my arms around them,
since I'm still wearing shorts.

We sit there, listening to the birds
somewhere behind us, until
Mr. Langley says, *I grew up
without a daddy.* He's staring
at the building, even though
we're facing a side that hasn't

been painted even a little bit.
It's the side he wants us to
paint together, but I haven't
gotten my side right yet.

He left right after my brother
was born. Mr. Langley clears his throat.
I guess I hated my brother for a while
after that.

His words make me think of Aunt Bee
and how her daddy turned nice,
which really means he quit drinking,
after her brother was born.
Mama once said Aunt Bee hated
my daddy for that, too.
But I don't say anything.

I lost my way for a while,
Mr. Langley says into my silence.
It's hard to know how to be a man
without a daddy.

My nose starts burning,
like my heart walked right up into it,

since Mr. Langley
has somehow seen the deepest hole in me
even though no one else could.

SWINGING

Mr. Langley is quiet for a long time,
so it's only the wind we hear now,
whistling through the spaces
we can't see.

There are other ways to figure out
how to be a man, Mr. Langley says finally.
He pulls a piece of grass and strips it
clear down the middle. *There are other*
men we can watch, men we want to be like.
He looks toward the building again.
My brother figured it out. And he was
that man for me.

What happened to him?
I can't stop the question.
I don't tell him I know
his brother was Greg's daddy.
Maybe he wants
it to be a secret.

Mr. Langley takes so long to answer
I think maybe he's not going to.
But then he says, *He died in that*
building right there.

He tells me about his brother,
who came back from the war and
took a temporary position
doing maintenance at the school
and every day stepped in and
out of the doors while
people threw things at his back.

At first I think maybe Mr. Langley
wanted to paint pictures on this building
to remember his brother, but then
he tells me about his brother's son
walking into the building one day after school,
even though he didn't go to this school then,
and seeing his daddy swinging from a rope,
how the boy screamed all the way
down the road and
all the way back.

Why did he do it? I say.

Mr. Langley stares at the
empty wall.
He didn't, he says.
He clears his throat.

Then how . . . I let
the words trail off.

Mr. Langley shakes his head.
Some people will do anything
to keep a black man
away from their white kids, he says.
Even if he's only a maintenance man.

HOPE

After that we don't say anything
for a good long while.

I think I understand now why
Mr. Langley wanted to paint this building
with a memory that was better
than the one it hid inside.

Come with me, Mr. Langley says,
and he's on his feet, heading out
to a field behind the building.
It's a whole field of blue and red flowers,
their faces turned up toward the sun.
*After he died, I used to come out here
and rest with the flowers,* Mr. Langley says.
He loved the Indian paintbrushes best.

He lies down on his back, and I do, too,
and then we're staring at the sky
through the petals of glowing flowers,
and I can't explain it, but it feels like
they're telling me something.

Mr. Langley looks at me,
like he understands. He smiles

and says, *This is hope,* and I feel
the warmth of his words reach
all the way to my toes.

MEMORY

I'm walking around after school
with nothing to do, wandering down
toward Greg's house without
even noticing, when I feel
the first drop of rain.

I don't think anything of it at first.
The sun is still out
and there aren't many clouds
and the sky still looks blue
from where I stand. But then
it happens fast, the whole day
darkening like the black clouds
were just waiting for permission
to take the light, and before I
can even think what to do,
the sky dumps water
all over me.

It's the first time since school started
that it's rained, and for some reason,
even though I thought I was better,
I can't move. My legs feel stiff,
like the cold water has somehow
glued my feet to the sidewalk.

And in all those drops I see
red and blue flashes
coloring our drive, and I hear gravel
crackling under tires louder
than the thunder in the distance,
and I see Mama fall to her knees
and Aunt Bee touch her soggy hair
and Gran running across the yard
without her shoes on.

EYES

Then I see Greg,
right in front of me.

He holds his arms out,
like he's trying to reach
for something I can't see.
His face is turned toward
the sky, and the drops
run down his mouth and
nose and chin.

I don't know why,
but I feel myself move now,
straight toward him.
He must know I'm coming,
since he says, *You want to*
wait out the storm on my porch?

I don't answer. He opens his eyes
and moves toward the covered place
where I saw his mama twice before.
I follow him.
He sits in one chair,
and I sit in another.

It took me a while to love
the rain again, Greg says.
He stares out toward the street and continues.
My daddy died on a day like this one.
He looks at me with eyes
blacker than the sky, and I stare
right back. He nods, like he
understands what I can't say.

SHOWER

We sit there for a while, not talking,
just listening to the rain thunder
on cement. Then he says, *It doesn't*
have to remind you of the worst day.
You can let it remind you of the
good ones that hide behind that
worst one. He turns to me again.
My uncle told me that.

The words are like
a secret door opening.
I remember the storm
that cracked and roared
and brought my daddy to the room
where me and Charlie couldn't sleep
and he curled up on the floor
so we wouldn't have to be alone.
I remember the time I stood by the
water's edge deep in the woods
and the rain came unexpected like today
and the woods turned night
and my daddy showed up
with a flashlight to lead me back home.
I remember all those days we spent
in his work shed, when he was

sculpting wood while I watched
and the rain tapped the roof
faster than his hammer
could tap in nails.

Come on, Greg says, and he
grabs my arm and pulls me out
into the pouring rain. He stands where
he was when I first saw him today
and stretches his arms out again.
He only looks at me for a second
before he says, *The rain can
clear away the worst memories.
My uncle told me that, too,*
and then he closes his eyes and
lifts his face back toward the sky.

And I guess it's worth a try,
so I do the same.

The water runs down my cheeks
and my neck
and my chest and back,
but it doesn't feel so cold anymore.
It feels warm, like a gentle shower.

So I let it in,
let it wash clean
the worst memory.
It clears away the shadows
hiding all the
good ones.

COOKIE

Greg sits with me
at lunch today.

It's the first time anyone
has even walked close to
my table, and something
about it makes me want to cry.

Want a cookie? Greg says,
holding out one with so many chips
it's more chocolate than cookie.
I packed two today.

Thanks, I say.
He shrugs.

We have them all the time, he says.
Mama still likes to bake, even though . . .
He doesn't finish his thought, just
takes a big bite of his peanut butter
and jam sandwich, probably so he
doesn't have to talk.

ARMOR

After a few minutes, when it looks
like he's chewed the whole bite,
I say, *What happened to her?*

Greg looks at me. I guess
he doesn't know I know, since he
never saw me those days I saw her.
So it's my turn to shrug.
I saw you playing
basketball one time, I say.
She was watching from the porch.

He doesn't answer my question,
but he does say, *Me and Daddy*
used to play basketball all the time.
He stares at his carrots, cut into rings.
He played in the pros before the war.
I think he wanted me to play, too.
He made me practice all the time.

Do you like basketball? I say.

He shakes his head. *I never liked it*
as much as he wanted me to, he says.
He turns a red apple over in his hands.

I think that made him sad.

I don't know what to say,
so I eat the rest of my sandwich
and the potato chips Aunt Bee
bought in bulk last week. We don't
say anything for the rest of lunch,
just sit there eating while the hum
of all the other voices rises and falls
around us. Then the bell rings and we
throw away our trash and start toward
the double doors where kids are
piling up. On our way through, Greg says,
The doctors don't really know what's
wrong with her. The disease took
her legs first. They don't know
what it will take next.

He's staring straight ahead,
closed tight where a minute ago
he had opened. And the way he
clamps shut makes me think this is
another way we're the same,
both of us carrying around
hard shells, armor protecting

all the parts of life we don't
understand and can't talk about.

I don't know what comes over me,
but I squeeze his shoulder like my
daddy used to do when I felt
disappointed or sad or just plain
confused. It's the first time I've
touched him with kind hands.

WINTER 1972-73

PROMISE

I don't notice that worry
darkens Aunt Bee's eyes
until we're all sitting around
a table of take-out pizza.
I look at the two boxes
and I have a feeling we're not
going to eat it once she says
what she needs to say.

The sky is like one of her paintings
outside the window, so I try to look
at it and not Aunt Bee's face.

Red and orange and yellow and green
and blue reach through the windows.
Gran once told me that
a promise of protection
was wrapped in a rainbow's colors.
But this one must be different.

UNFOLD

Aunt Bee waits until we
fill our plates with pizza before
she says, *I got something
from your mama today.*
She holds up two
folded pieces of paper.
Letters, she says.
She hands one to me
and one to Charlie.

I forget all about my pizza.

I take my letter and run out the front door,
to the shadows and the cold
where they can't see me while I read it.
I glance back at the house.
Charlie and Aunt Bee stand on the porch.
Charlie's hands are on her face.

Charlie must have read her letter.
I unfold mine and stare at Mama's words
that start shaking before I'm even
done.

STAY

Dear Paulie, Mama writes.
I know you kids don't understand
why I left like I did.
If I told you it was because I needed
to get better, you'd ask
better from what,
and that's all too much
to explain in a letter. But I do
want you to know I'm better.
I'm ready to be the mama
you need again.

She says she wants to take
me and Charlie away so we can
make a new life together. She says
there's someone she wants us to meet,
someone who loves her and loves us already,
someone who will make us a family again.
She says she loves me, and then she
signs her name instead of *Mama.*
Probably just habit.

There's a P.S. at the bottom of the letter,
scribbled in a different color pen,
like maybe it was added later.

Be sure and tell Bee thank you, it says.
For watching over both of you
while I was gone.

I fold the letter again
and put it in my pocket.
I stand and stare at the
biggest house I've ever lived in
for the happiest time of my life
with one of the best people
I've ever known.

I don't want to leave.
I don't, I don't, I don't.

I hope Mama changes her mind.
I hope she lets us stay.
I hope she goes away
and never comes back.

I see Aunt Bee move.
Charlie falls into her arms.
I sink to the street, alone.
The whole world blurs.

KILLERS

When I finally went inside last night,
it was all over the news,
how the police
found my daddy's killers.
The news reporters called it
just another casualty of the race war,
and Aunt Bee cursed at the screen
before she saw me and tried to
switch the channel real quick.
But I saw my daddy's killers,
looking ugly and mean.
Some policemen shoved them
into cars and drove them away.
I didn't say anything
on the way to my room.

CHOOSE

Today I'm back in Mrs. Walsh's office.

I heard you got a letter,
Mrs. Walsh says, closing
the door behind me.

I try to feel as excited
about Mama's letter as
Mrs. Walsh seems to feel,
but so much hangs
around my neck that I don't
even know if I can smile.
Yeah, I say.

She sits behind her desk
and leans forward. *Tell me, Paulie,*
she says. *How do you feel about it?*
Getting a letter from your mama, I mean.

I don't say anything. I can't.

Mrs. Walsh looks at me
for a long time, and then she says,
Maybe you're afraid and
a little shocked. Maybe even mad.

She twists her hands together
and sets them on top of her calendar,
open to this week's pages. *It was all
so sudden and unexpected. I know
it's scary not knowing what's next.*

She's walking around in my head,
and I don't know how she got there,
being as I haven't opened the door.

*I just want you to know that
you have a choice,* Mrs. Walsh says.
*You can choose to stay or you can
choose to go.*

My stomach knots tighter.

Does she think it feels better
knowing this? Now, no matter what
I choose, I'm disappointing someone.

PICTURE

Mrs. Walsh leans forward again
so she can pat my hand. *You don't*
have to make a decision today or
tomorrow or even next week, she says.
You can take as long as you need.
She turns toward her bag.
In the meantime, look at this.
She pulls out a picture of water,
surrounded by trees. It's the place
where me and my daddy used to fish.
How does she know about our place?

When I look at her, she shrugs.
I live on the other side, she says.
I heard it was a special place for you.

It was special before my daddy left.
We would talk about art
and dreams and music.
I loved my daddy most in that place,
even more than I loved him in his shed
making furniture or under the tree
sitting beside me.

I take the picture and
stare at it for a long time.
Mrs. Walsh clears her throat.
When you feel confused, just
pull out the picture, she says.
And then imagine who you'd
want to stand there next to you now.

She opens the door and I'm out
and Greg's in before I can even
find my voice to say thank you.
I put the picture in my back pocket
and feel it there all the way
to class.

ROSE

I follow Greg home
from school today.

I think Aunt Bee is happy
I have something to do
on the days me and
Mr. Langley don't paint,
but I think she's mostly happy
I have a friend.

If I'm being honest,
I'm happy I have
a friend, too.

Greg doesn't bring up Mama
on the way, even though
he knows about the letter
and the choice I'll
have to make soon.

For a long time,
the only sound between us
is the wind shaking the trees
and our feet clapping the sidewalk.

What would you do? I finally say
when we're halfway to his house.

He seems to know
what I'm talking about,
since he says, *You mean*
if I was you?

I nod and wait.

He stares out at the houses we pass,
and then he says, *Hang on.*
I watch him run up the driveway of one,
stop at a bush exploding with bright pink roses,
and race back to me with one stem
and a bud in his hand.

They'll never miss one, he says,
and he pushes the rose to his nose.
Mama loves roses. Daddy used to
bring her great big piles of them
every week. His voice is sad
and full of memories and maybe a
streak of anger, too.

HERE

Greg doesn't take long to find
his way back to my question.
On the one hand, he says, *you have*
a good home now. Mrs. Adams loves you.
You eat good food you don't have to cook.
You have a friend.
Greg kicks a rock
that's out of place on our path.
He doesn't look at me, just stares
at the black driveway we're crossing
and keeps talking. *On the other hand,*
she's your mama.

I don't know what to do, I say,
and my eyes turn blurry.

Greg stops and puts his hand
on my shoulder. *You don't want to*
disappoint either of them, he says.
It's not a question. He says it like
he knows and understands.

Then he tells me about the time
after his daddy died, when his mama
started dropping things and tripping

and spending whole days in bed on account of
her legs being so numb. His uncle wanted
to take him for a while, until they could
figure things out, and he had to make
a decision like mine.

I want to ask him how he made his choice,
except before I can, he drops
the rose in his hand and races up
the stairs of the porch. The only words
he says are, *She's not here.*

BRAVE

I follow Greg inside,
panic filling my mouth
for reasons I don't understand.
I call his name, but someone
else is calling him, too, and he
doesn't hear me.

Mama! he screams, tearing through the rooms.
She's on the white floor of a bathroom.
Her face is twisted and looks
like dead ashes after a fire,
but she smiles when she sees him.
I'm okay, she says. *I fell on my way out.*
She looks at me, her eyes seeing
something beyond me. *Sorry your*
new friend has to see me like this.

I watch Greg try to lift her up,
his feet nearly stumbling, and I move
to her other side so I can help, too.
Greg clicks on the brakes of her chair
and we set his mama gently in the seat.
And it's then that I understand.

Greg picked her.
He picked this.
He chose a life taking care
of someone else over a life
where someone took care of him.

I wish I could be
so brave.

LOST

We don't talk much during the
rest of my stay. We just watch the
small television in a family room
that is almost bare except for a
battered brown couch and
a couple of bookshelves.
His mama offers us cookies.
I take two, but Greg
waves them away.
When she smiles into my eyes,
I see only deep holes of sadness.

My fingers on the side of the couch
tap out all the questions
I want to ask Greg but can't.
How often does she fall?
Does he regret his decision?
Would he make a different one if he
could have seen today and all the
other days like it?

Greg keeps a hand over his mouth,
like he wants me to know this isn't
open for discussion.

And then it's time to leave,
and he's walking me to the door,
saying, *Just don't tell,*
and I'm nodding okay.

The last thing I see,
after I've waved to them
both on the porch, is the
bright pink rose, dropped
in the middle of their driveway,
its petals scattered like all the pieces
of Greg's life he lost
so he could choose his mama.

SINGING

Aunt Bee is out tending flowers,
even though it's dark.
She stays out until it's time
to tell us good night.

I like to watch her
on the nights she sings.
She hasn't been singing since
Mama sent us our letters, though.
I miss her singing. I want
to hear her voice again, and I think this
might be why I open the door and
walk down the porch steps and
stand by her side tonight.

The flowers look pretty, I say,
just to let her know I'm here.

She turns her face to me and smiles,
but her eyes stay tight and dark,
like they don't remember
how to smile the way the rest
of her face does. She moves her hand
under one of the white flowers
we thought for sure wouldn't make it.

She bends to smell it.
I didn't think I'd ever see this one
bloom again, she says. *Your gran's got*
magic in her hands.

Her voice is sad and happy
at the same time. I touch
the velvety petals of the bloom
closest to me, and she sits back
on her heels.

Your daddy gave it to me,
and I let it die, she says.
Her eyes are like brown
pieces of glass, but she blinks
the shine away. And then,
so soft I can hardly hear,
she says, *And here it is again.*
Resurrected.

I let her have her quiet for a minute,
but there's something I need to say,
something that's been burning up
inside of me since reading Mama's letter.
I don't really know how to say it, so

I count a minute and then I blurt out,
I don't want to go back,
before I lose my nerve.

Aunt Bee doesn't say anything at all.
She just folds me in her arms
and lets me stay.

After a long breath,
she starts singing.

STORM

Aunt Bee pulls me from class
three hours before the last school bell.
She tells me we're going to a hospital,
but she doesn't say why.

We stop to get Charlie on the way.
Aunt Bee parks close to a sidewalk
darkened by trees and tells me
to wait in the car while she goes in.
So I wait, staring out the windows
at a bright blue sky with a few
puffy clouds, nothing to warn
about a storm coming.

It doesn't look like the kind of day
something would go wrong, but
I know how pretty days can trick us
with their sunshine and
clear skies.

KNOW

There is an old tree,
off to the side of the street,
with branches that twist
all the way up to the sun and
leaves that let light through.
It's tall and wide and strong,
and for some reason, it makes me
think of Granddad.

Charlie slides into the front seat
beside Aunt Bee. She looks back
at me with all kinds of questions
in her eyes, the same ones trying
to climb out of my mouth.

I don't know any more
than Charlie does.

All I know is Aunt Bee stops
by her house but doesn't go in,
just picks all the white flowers
from the plant my daddy
gave her.

All I know is she drives faster
than she's ever driven before,
flying around other cars and
cursing under her breath when
she gets blocked in, more like Gran
today than she's ever been.

All I know is she tells me and Charlie
to wait in a too-bright room while
she takes those flowers into a
hallway marked ICU
and disappears for a long time.

I fall asleep
on a cushioned chair
with wooden arms.

DIE

When I wake up, it's Aunt Bee
who is sleeping in a chair next to me.
Charlie stands by the window.
I slide out of my chair, careful
not to disturb Aunt Bee, and
walk over to Charlie. She's staring
out at the sidewalk, and it doesn't
take long to see why.

All over the gray stone
are the flowers Aunt Bee brought.
I don't know how they got there.

She threw them out, Charlie says.

My heart sounds loud
in my ears. It must be
worse than I thought.

He's not dead, Charlie says,
and for a minute I think she might be
talking about my daddy, except I
saw the crumpled car and I heard the shots
and I felt the cold that every boy must feel
when their daddy leaves them.

Granddad, Charlie says.
She turns to me, her eyes like
the deep end of an ocean.
He's just not exactly alive, either.

I don't know what this means,
not being exactly alive. So, I ask,
Will he die, then?

Charlie turns back toward the window,
toward all those flowers that
look like death, now that I know.
I don't want to see them pointing
the way inside this place
where people come to die.

HEART

He hasn't woken up yet, that's all.
It's not Charlie who answers
my question. It's Aunt Bee.
She stands right behind us now.
We'll know more when he wakes up.

She tells us how he was out pulling weeds,
trying to gather what vegetables he could
before the first freeze came in, and then he
fell over on his back, so numb he
couldn't even move. Gran was
out with him and saw it happen,
and that's the only reason he didn't
show up at the hospital already dead.

He had a heart attack, she says.
And they got his heart working again,
but no one really knows what
happens from here. She sounds bitter,
like she blames him for the heart attack.

I don't know what comes
over me, but I say, *Why did you*
throw all those flowers away?

Aunt Bee looks at me
for a long time. And then I guess
she decides to tell the truth.
She says, *If he dies,*
I won't be able to tell him
something I've waited to
tell him for years.

I almost ask what that something is,
but the way her mouth twists
keeps me quiet instead.

Tears roll down her cheeks,
and me and Charlie don't know
what else to do. We both
take one of her hands and hold her
for as long as it takes.

I guess this is what you do
when you know what it's like
to lose a daddy.

PETALS

Later, when Aunt Bee has
fallen asleep in her chair again
and Charlie is down in the dining hall
getting supper, I walk out the
sliding doors and collect all
the white petals that
haven't blown away.

Granddad might still
want them, after all.
A present from his two kids,
one dead and one
still alive.

FLOWERS

On the fifth day,
Granddad wakes up.

It happens fast.
Gran comes running
out the same door
Aunt Bee ran in five days ago.
She looks smaller and older
and too tired for words.
She waves Aunt Bee toward her,
and Aunt Bee pats Charlie's knee
and tells us she'll be right back,
and then she disappears and
we're waiting again, not knowing
what's happened.

Then she's back, and
me and Charlie are walking
through the doors we haven't
been allowed through in all the days
we've sat in a waiting area with
three hundred and ninety-six circles
on the carpet, and we stop at a room
with an open door and a heavy smell
like old people mixed with soap and

something I might call death, if
Aunt Bee wasn't still smiling.

I must be wrong.

She walks behind us into the room,
and the first thing I see is a clear vase
of yellow flowers on a windowsill,
and I wonder how they got here
and who might have sent them.

They're the same flowers
Mama used to keep on our
kitchen table. That's the
only reason I wonder.

PLAN

Granddad is sitting up in bed
with four pillows behind his back,
blinking in the light from the window.

Charlie moves to Granddad's side,
so I do the same. He says something
I can't understand.
I look at Aunt Bee, wondering if
it's just me. She's standing right
behind me, still smiling.

She leans toward me.
He's a strong one, she says.
He'll find his words again.
Just let him talk if he wants.

I don't know how Granddad
could have lost his words,
but nothing he says
sounds like sentences
or conversation at all.
Charlie takes his hand, but I
keep my distance.

He's still a little confused, Gran says.
She stands up and touches his forehead,
moving her hand all the way across
the crinkled paper of his skin.
It might take a few days.

Granddad leans his head back
on the pillow and closes his eyes.
Aunt Bee says it's time to go.
She moves to Granddad's side and
whispers words, but I hear them all.
I'll be back tomorrow, Daddy.
We have so much to
talk about.

Me and Charlie follow her
out of the room and out the doors
marked ICU and all the way
out the front of the hospital.
And even though it's our first day
going home after five days of
sleeping in a hospital waiting room,
I don't think about home
or a hot bath or how good
my own bed will feel tonight.

I only think about how I want
to hear what Aunt Bee
will say to Granddad.

VISITOR

When we get home,
a car I've never seen
is parked out front.
It's a bright orange Ford Pinto.
The only reason I know
is on account of Mama laughing
with my daddy one time when we
passed *such an ugly car* on the highway.

Aunt Bee stands outside her
car door for a minute, and
I swear her face turns younger
in the golden light.

Charlie looks at me, wondering
the same thing I'm wondering.
I shrug. We follow Aunt Bee
around the corner to the porch.
Mr. Langley is rocking
back and forth in the chair
Aunt Bee usually sits in.

Luke, Aunt Bee says.
I've never heard her call him
anything but Mr. Langley.

I stare at her, and I guess
my mouth must be open,
since Charlie elbows me.
I look at Mr. Langley
just long enough to
see him wink.

I came as soon as I heard,
Mr. Langley says. *But you
weren't home. So I kept trying.*

We were staying at the hospital,
Aunt Bee says, and her voice
holds a hundred yawns.
I yawn, too.

He woke up, then, Mr. Langley says.
He starts to take her hand,
but Aunt Bee waves us all
through the front door.

We'll talk inside, she says,
and I know what she means is
away from me and Charlie.

DOORWAY

Mr. Langley is the last one
through the door. Me and Charlie
go straight to our rooms,
but we'll be back.
We wouldn't miss their talk
for all the sleep we might get
in our own beds before supper.

So we wait. And when we hear
the pots and pans clanging
in the kitchen, we sneak out
with socks and silent steps.

I barely breathe, peering around
the doorway. Mr. Langley's hand
is on Aunt Bee's arm.
He pulls her close
and wraps his arms around her.
I'm so glad he made it, he says.
His voice is ancient and sad,
like it's been around for
a thousand years, but it's still
bright at the edges.

Aunt Bee buries her face
in his shoulder and doesn't
say anything. They stay that way
for a long time, until Aunt Bee
pulls away and turns back to the stove.
She wipes the back of her hand
across her eyes, like she might be
getting rid of tears.

Mr. Langley pushes himself onto
the counter beside the stove,
like my daddy used to do.
He watches Aunt Bee turn on
the burners and break apart spaghetti
and drop it into the water. He lets her
stay in her quiet until she hands him
the sauce jar and he twists it open
in one try.
Then he says, *When will you
talk to him?*

Aunt Bee stirs the spaghetti pot
and says, *As soon as he'll understand,*
and her voice breaks apart
in the middle of it.

It's then I realize how scared
she is that Granddad will never
get better. That he will never
understand.

Mr. Langley slides off the counter
and puts his arms around Aunt Bee
again. *I'm ready to marry you,* he says,
real quiet. But me and Charlie
hear it easily, since we've listened
to talking softer than those words.
I've been ready a long time.

I know, Aunt Bee says.
She looks him straight in the eye.
*I am, too. But I have to make it right
with Daddy first.*

Of course, Mr. Langley says.
There's so much to say.
So much for him
to make right, too.

Aunt Bee nods, and she has that
look on her face like she can't

talk anymore. After a minute, Mr. Langley
kisses her right on the mouth.

Charlie gasps. We have sense enough
to move back into the living room
and then race real quiet back
to her room.

COMPLICATED

I sit on Charlie's bed.
Charlie stares out her window,
into the backyard where Milo
used to play. The sun
colors her hair orange,
and the blinds turn
her face zebra.

I told you, she says.
They love each other.

I'm still trying to process
what I've seen, but I know
enough to know she's right.

*Why can't they just
marry each other, then?* I say.

*I reckon because she's white
and he's black,* Charlie says.
People don't like that sort of thing.
Charlie turns to me.
*But that doesn't mean
they won't get married.*
She's smiling.

Golden hands reach through
Charlie's window, and I can feel
their warmth from the top of my head
all the way to my toes.

MIXING

Aunt Bee says we're not
going to the hospital today,
since Granddad is tired.
We go to school instead.
So I go see Mr. Langley.

We haven't painted
the building since
Granddad's heart attack, and I still
need to finish my field
before we start on the wall
we're supposed to paint together.

Mr. Langley is standing
at the back of his room,
near the washing-up sink.
He looks up when I come in,
and his face folds into a smile.

Paulie, he says,
like I'm just the person
he wanted to see.
His words warm me
like Mama's smile always did.

I came to see if
we could paint, I say.
Granddad's too tired
for a visit today.

Mr. Langley dips the brushes in
one side of the sink and pours
a measuring cup of gray water
down the other.

Help me finish these, he says,
without saying whether we'll
paint today. So I stand beside him,
handing him measuring cups and
stirring spoons and other things
I don't know the names of.
There are whole stacks of
paint-splattered things.

We're learning how to
mix colors, Mr. Langley says,
like he knows I'm wondering
about the mess. *The younger*
students don't know as much as
students like you.

We're quiet for a few minutes,
pouring out and washing and
making new and cleaner stacks,
and I'm thinking about the other night,
when he sat through supper with us
and no one said a word about
how weird it was, how he stayed
to help Aunt Bee wash all the dishes
after me and Charlie had gone back
to our rooms, how I saw him
kiss her again right before
he left.

And I guess my brain forgets
all about keeping my thoughts
safe and private, since I say,
You've never come over before.

Mr. Langley doesn't say anything
for a while, just keeps wiping
a soapy sponge over the cups.

COLORS

Finally, when no more dishes wait for washing
and the drain has sucked all the water down,
Mr. Langley wipes his hands on his pants
and turns to face me.
Your aunt and I . . . , he says,
and then he stops.

I wait.

I asked her to marry me once, Mr. Langley says.
He turns back to the sink, even though
nothing else is there. *She said no.*
I never really got over it.

He stares out the only window
in the room, right above the sink.
I'm not tall enough to see what
holds him there, so I look at his hands,
gripping the counter in a way
that turns his knuckles almost white.
I blurt out, *Why?*

Why indeed, he says.
He draws a deep breath.
Some people don't like to mix colors.

He looks at me again.
Bee has a father.
A father with opinions.

His words grab me by the throat.
That's just stupid, I say.
She loves you.
You love her.
And she's all grown up.
What does it matter what Grandad thinks?

Mr. Langley smiles,
but his eyes are sad. *Well, maybe this time*
will work, then, is all he says.

We stand there and let
time tick through our thoughts,
until the sun comes blasting
into our eyes and we both realize
there's no time left for painting.

It's probably time for you to go,
Mr. Langley says, his hand on my shoulder.
We'll paint every day you don't go
to the hospital. I promise.

I look into his face, shiny and
still young-looking, even though
his hair is gray at the sides,
and I know, for once,
that I can trust the promises
someone makes.

Mr. Langley is nothing
like my daddy.

CHANGING

The whole world
is changing.

I see it in the trees
that wore gold and rust
and pumpkin yesterday
but are wearing nothing today.
I feel it in the way
Aunt Bee drives to the
hospital this afternoon,
all careful and calm and
too slow, if you ask me.
I hear it in her footsteps down the hall,
in her voice calling hello
to all the nurses she's never really
noticed before.

It almost makes me go back to
Charlie and the empty waiting room,
since there's no telling when
she'll turn around and notice
that I'm not where I'm
supposed to be.

But I make it to Granddad's room,
behind her, without being seen.

I press my back against the wall
beside the door.

How is he today? Aunt Bee says.

He can answer for himself, Granddad says.
His voice sounds rough and scratchy,
like he hasn't used it in too long.

You're back, Aunt Bee says,
and I don't even have to look.
I can hear the smile in her voice.

But I look anyhow.
She bends to hug
Granddad's neck.

I'm back, he grumbles.
I never went anywhere.

Gran pats his head,
and they all talk for too long
about little things, like the weather
and school and traffic
on the drive up.

I stop listening for a minute,
until I hear Aunt Bee say,
There's something I need to say,
and my feet freeze solid
to the ground.

It's quiet for only a second
before Granddad says,
Well, then say it.

I'm getting married, she says,
and I press my hand to my mouth,
but it doesn't stop the giant smile
from opening my mouth.
Gran and Granddad stare at her
with their mouths wide-open, too,
but I can't really tell if they're happy
or really shocked.
I'm marrying Lucas Langley.
Aunt Bee looks down at her hands.
He asked me years ago,
but you let me know how you felt
about men like him.
She looks at Granddad.
He only grunts.

Men like him? Gran says.

Aunt Bee hasn't stopped
looking at Granddad.
Her face holds the pain of a
hundred years it seems.
I feel sorry for her.
Black men, she says.
Black men who love
white women.

HEAVY

The room gets really quiet,
so I try not to even breathe,
afraid they'll hear me
outside the door.

I love him, Aunt Bee says.
I have for a very long time.
She looks from one to the other,
Gran and then Granddad
and then back to Gran.
I can't put my life on hold
any longer so you can be
all right with my choice.

She lets the sentence trail off,
and no one talks for
a long time.

Finally, Granddad says,
I should never have forbidden it,
and even from here, I can see
the way his eyes turn to glass.
Aunt Bee takes his hand.
Just because of your ex-husband.
Just because of a child.

He swallows hard.
Just because of his skin color.
He shakes his head. *It didn't mean . . .*
His voice breaks, and then
everyone is crying loud,
great, heaving sobs
so I have to turn away
or I might, too.

I guess they've all been holding
heavy things inside for too long.

I should have let you raise your son,
Granddad says. His voice cracks
all around the words. *I should have
told him who you were instead of
lying to him his whole life.*

My face starts to feel warm.
I can't really say why. I just
have this feeling I know who
they're talking about.

*You were better parents to John Paul
than I could have been,* Aunt Bee says.

I was too young to be a mother. It took me
too long to find my feet after his daddy left.
You did my son a favor
taking him like you did.
What kind of life would
I have given him?

I don't hear anything else after that,
on account of the whole world
humming loud like my daddy
used to do when he didn't want
to hear what Mama had to say,
when she would turn away with
anger squeezing all the
muscles around her mouth.

John Paul was
my daddy's name.

John Paul wasn't
Aunt Bee's brother.

John Paul was
Aunt Bee's son.

The whole world is changing.
I hear it in the buzzing that closes up
my ears and shakes into my throat.
I feel it in the freezing fingers
that grip my chest and
my arms and my legs.
I see it in the floor reaching up
to meet my cheek.

And then all the
world's colors
turn black.

ANSWERS

I don't know
what to call her.

She is my grandmother,
but she is Aunt Bee.

She is Aunt Bee,
with her black-and-white hair,
and eyes that watch my every move,
and arms that have started
to feel like home.

She is the mama of my daddy,
the one who picked up
all the pieces when
Mama dropped them.

She is our mama and our daddy
and our aunt and our grandmother,
and I don't know what to call her.

She sits beside me at the table outside,
watching the trees bend in today's wind.
It's cold, so I have a heavy jacket on.
My sketchbook stares at me,

a blank page ready, but I can't
think of anything to draw.

Aunt Bee or another
name completely?

That day at the hospital,
all Aunt Bee's secrets came out.
My daddy was her son.
Gran and Granddad took him in
after Aunt Bee's husband left her
and she couldn't find a job.
Gran and Granddad
raised my daddy like he was
her brother instead of her son.

He didn't know.

When Mr. Langley asked Aunt Bee
to marry him back when my daddy
was my age, Aunt Bee said no.
But not because she
didn't love Mr. Langley.
It was because Granddad told her
that if she married Mr. Langley,

she could forget about seeing her son.
He said he didn't want his daughter
marrying another good-for-nothing artist,
but what he really meant
was he didn't want her marrying
a black man.

It makes sense now, how Granddad
wouldn't set foot inside Aunt Bee's house,
how Aunt Bee hid all her art, on principle.
The way Aunt Bee spent all her free time
at our house, helping Mama and
cooking dinner and tucking
my daddy in when he was
too far gone to do it himself.
The angry twist of her mouth,
not meant for my daddy but for
Granddad and the secret
he made her keep.

She gave up her son,
her painting, and
her future because of
Granddad.

They've been fighting
for a long, long time.

TRUTH

Aunt Bee told us why my daddy
killed the man in the bar, too.
I guess once secrets start coming out
they all get easier to tell.

My daddy's best friend, Dave,
went on record to say the bartender
at the bar he and my daddy went to
the night my daddy died
refused to give Dave a drink
on account of his skin color.
The bartender was a white man.
My daddy told him,
Well, that ain't right.
Black men deserve a drink
just the same as any white man.
What's it matter what color his skin is?

This made some other
white men in the bar mad.
The bartender told my daddy
and Dave to leave the bar,
since he didn't want any trouble.
But my daddy made
trouble anyway.

Some friends of the bartender
threatened Dave, said they'd
kill him if he didn't get on out
and find himself a bar
that served his kind.
Aunt Bee said they'd probably
had too much to drink,
and that's why they talked about killing.
But her eyes looked like
she didn't quite believe it.

One of the white men
pulled a gun and pointed it at Dave,
and my daddy snapped, beat him up,
and then ran for his life.
Dave found my daddy's tangled-up car
and the holes in his chest
and then he ran, too,
without telling anybody what he saw,
since he knew exactly what the police
would think if they found him beside
a white man who'd been shot.

Dave was my daddy's
best friend. My daddy died
defending his best friend.

It feels good to know that.

SIT

No picture today?
Aunt Bee says.

I shake my head.
Can't think of anything, I say.
Except black-and-white curls
and brown eyes and a mouth
that smiles much more
than it used to.

She's quiet for a few minutes,
and the wind shakes the tree
above us so a dried-out leaf falls
on the table. She stares at it.
Nothing has to change, she says,
like she knows what might be
keeping me from drawing.
I can still be your aunt Bee.
She looks at me. *I don't mind.*
If you don't.

Next thing I know, I'm nodding,
saying, *Okay, I'll still call you Aunt Bee,*
and it feels right. Good. Special, even.
She smiles at me, and I can feel it

in my chest and my stomach
and my feet.

There are still so many questions
I'd like to ask and so many stories
I'd like to hear, but I'll save them
for another day.

Today, I will just sit
on the back porch
with my aunt Bee.

GIFT

We're all gathered in
Gran and Granddad's living room.
Granddad has finally come home.

Gran is flying around the kitchen,
checking the turkey and stirring
mashed potatoes and frying up
her okra. Me and Charlie
sit in the living room with
Aunt Bee and Mr. Langley
and Greg, waiting.

Greg had to move in
with Mr. Langley a week ago,
on account of his mama
getting worse.

Mama couldn't be here,
even though it's Christmas.

She wrote us a long letter
and said she's trying to get back
on her feet and she's finally got
a decent job, so she can't take
time away just yet.

Aunt Bee says Mama is
trying hard to clean up her life.
I guess that's as good a
Christmas gift as any.

HUG

Even though two people
in my life are missing today,
this house still feels full.

Earlier, when we showed up
at the door, Granddad answered,
looking like his old self. He shook
Mr. Langley's hand, and then
he hugged him.

I don't think I ever saw
Granddad hug my daddy.
Aunt Bee's face looked just like
the sun, it was shining so bright.

BROTHER

How much longer? I say to Gran,
stepping inside a kitchen
that makes my stomach rumble.

A few more minutes, she says.

A few more minutes to Gran
means at least twenty.
I learned that a long time ago.
So I take Greg outside to show him
Granddad's garden.

It isn't as pretty as it
used to be, since Granddad
was in the hospital for so long.
The doctors told him not to work
so hard in the garden, but that's
where he says he wants to die.
He probably will, too.

Me and Greg walk to the end
of the driveway. Someone
paved the road in front of
Gran's house in the months
me and Charlie have been gone.

It's so foggy out I can't see
Brian's house at the end.
That's okay, though. I still
miss my old friend,
but I have a new one.
I look at Greg beside me.
He is like me in so many ways,
and maybe that's why I love him
just like I would love a brother
if I had one.

CHRISTMAS

There is still a whole lot we don't know.
Will Granddad be able to make a spring garden?
Will Mama come back home, just when
we're getting used to a life without her?
Will Greg's mama die?

But today is Christmas,
and even though the next year
looks a lot like that road and
its thick fog, me and Greg
made a deal before we came here
not to talk or think about any of that.

Boys. Aunt Bee is standing on the porch,
one hand on her hip. Her hair is more
gray than black now, but she is still
pretty. *Time to eat.*

Me and Greg race back inside,
since we're both starving, and there's
not room enough at the table for us all,
so Gran lets us sit in the
living room instead.

It's the best Christmas lunch
I think I've ever had.

We open our gifts, new art supplies
for me, some books for Greg,
and stacks of violin music sheets
for Charlie, who has gotten good
without us even noticing.
After we've cleaned up the paper,
Gran pulls out her violin
and Aunt Bee sits at the piano
and Granddad picks up his old guitar,
and we sit around the tree
singing Christmas songs.
Aunt Bee's clear sweet voice meets
Mr. Langley's deep one that
can't hold a tune at all.
Me and Greg and Charlie
laugh to hear it,
but that doesn't stop him.

We sing until the sun is gone
and the tree lights make our
faces glow.

And then we eat pie
and cobbler and fudge
until our bellies ache.

ROAD

The road is foggier on our way home,
but, for some reason, the world
doesn't feel so foggy anymore.

I guess it doesn't really matter as much
what the future might be hiding,
since I have today.

We drive past the curve where
my daddy's car flipped off the road,
and I don't even close my eyes.
It's the first time I've watched it pass
since the night my daddy died.

SPRING 1973

MAMA

Today me and Greg
are graduating from
elementary school.

It feels like a gigantic step,
going to a brand-new school
where there will be no Aunt Bee
or Mr. Langley. It feels a little scary,
if I'm honest.

We sit up on a stage with
all the other fifth graders,
who probably feel excited and
scared at the same time, just like me.
The lights blur the audience,
but I know who's there.

Gran. Granddad.
Charlie. Mr. Langley.

And Mama.

She showed up right before
me and Greg had to get onstage.
I didn't know if she would come,

but she had to watch her boy
graduate, she said. She hugged me
close and kissed the top of my head.
I'm so proud of you, she said.
She smelled like cigarette smoke.

Greg looked away, but not before
I saw the water in his eyes.
Three months ago his mama
was moved to a home where
nurses can take care of her all the time.
He still gets really sad about it.
He misses her a bunch, especially
on days like today.

NAME

Greg sits two rows in front of me.
I listen to all the names called,
and when it's Greg's, I let out a whoop.
Someone in the audience does, too.

Greg is grinning when he
shakes Aunt Bee's hand and she
gives him the piece of paper that
says he has finished his time at
River Oaks Elementary.

Finally, it's my turn,
and I hear more whoops,
and Aunt Bee hugs me tight
and kisses my forehead,
just like Mama did, except
Aunt Bee smells like oranges and coconut.
Then she hands me my piece of paper.
I take it back to my seat and
spread it on my lap.

John Paul Sanders.

It was my daddy's name.
But it's my name, too,
and I am the one
left to carry it
into the future.

WALL

When it's all over and
most of the people have
disappeared from the auditorium,
Mr. Langley takes us back
to the building I painted with him.
We finished our walls
four weeks ago.

He leads us all to the wall
we painted together.

Everyone stands there, staring.
Aunt Bee's eyes fill and then
empty down the sides of her face.
Gran's mouth is open. Mama says,
Oh my God, over and over, and then,
It's absolutely beautiful.

It's Gran and Granddad's living room,
except it's wider, with more chairs,
enough for all the ones who've left us, too.
The forms don't have faces,
but we all know who they are.

There is no Christmas tree,
but there is light shining on all the faces,
so they look like they are not quite
in this world but halfway in another,
the one Gran's preacher used to talk about,
where no one ever dies and the sun
always shines and the mistakes
of the past are nothing more than
forgotten memories.

Mr. Langley smiles at me,
his hand squeezing my shoulder.
It was Paulie's idea, he says.

We let them stand there, staring,
taking it all in, imagining the place,
until someone's stomach grumbles
and someone else laughs, and then
we're all turning together toward the cars,
the last ones in the parking lot.

GOODBYE

I let Mama hold my hand
all the way to the car.
When we get there,
she kisses my cheek and
holds me tight again.
I love you, she says.
Her voice crumbles in the
middle of the words.
So much.

I love you, too, I say,
since I really, really do.
I have loved her all along,
even if I didn't want her to
come back and spoil everything.
I love her especially today,
since I know without her saying a word
that she won't be coming back to get us.

I love her for doing the hard thing.
I love her for letting me live my life.
I love her for knowing
that this is what I need.

She hugs Charlie, and then
she walks away with fast steps,
her heels clicking on the cement.

Thank you, Mama, I whisper.

I watch her disappear down the road,
and then my eye catches on a berry bunch
someone dropped on the cement.
The color, bright red on gray,
looks a whole lot like
my life today.

Gray was the old life,
the one where a daddy
disappeared and a mama left
and a boy walked around
with too many empty spaces
to fill again. I thought life
would always be gray.

I'm not saying life is perfect.
The protestors still shout awful things
at Mr. Langley and Greg when we
walk through the streets of our city.

People still fight one another for what
they think is right.

But my life today is mostly red,
with an aunt Bee and
an uncle Luke and
Gran and Granddad and
Greg and Charlie,
all different shades and colors
living together like family.
Like we were meant to be.

Sometimes family doesn't look
exactly the way we expect it to.
Sometimes it looks maybe
just a little bit better.

Author's Note

The Colors of the Rain began with a sentence: "I heard the shots from nine miles away." This sentence does not open the book, nor is it completely intact anywhere within it. But this sentence was important, because it was my first encounter with Paulie and his remarkable life.

While I have taken creative liberties with Paulie and his family's story, many of the circumstances surrounding him are true—the Houston Independent School District was somewhat behind in the integration of black students into its predominantly white schools. A very slow, nationwide desegregation began in 1954, after the historic U.S. Supreme Court case *Brown v. Board of Education*, which declared that all racial segregation (or separation of white students and black students) in public schools violated the U.S. Constitution's promise of equal rights and protection for all people. Several Southern states, particularly those where racial segregation was prominent, took more time to integrate than the national government believed they should.

The Colors of the Rain is my attempt to capture this piece of history alongside some of its emotional undertones. Desegregation was dangerous work, full of passionate protests, unthinkable violence, and both overt and covert racism. Desegregation was not an overnight success. It required decades of hard work, persistence, and conviction to integrate successfully—and even today, there exist places in the south, as well as the north, that still haven't fully embraced equal rights for all people, regardless of their skin tone, their culture, or their way of life. We often forget the painful and difficult work required to heal human divides—work that includes acceptance, understanding, and love.

It's important to remember.

There is still so much work to be done. One of the most important things we can do is what you have done with *The Colors of the Rain*: Listen to the stories of others.

It's not easy to understand those who bully. It's not easy to understand those who make bad choices. It's not easy to understand people who are different from us. But when we listen to their stories without assuming we already know who they are, based on what they do and how they live and what they look like, we have the greatest chance of healing the divides in our world. Of repairing what's been broken. Of living in love.

I hope you and I will be brave enough to do our part.

Acknowledgments

I always knew *The Colors of the Rain* would eventually be published, though it was a long and winding road that led to this book in your hands. Countless rejections, countless revisions, and countless people lead to a book's birth into the world. I'm so grateful that I don't have to walk this road alone.

Thank you, first and foremost, to my amazing husband, Ben, for taking the kids swimming or to the park or for just simply cooking dinner, even though it's not your night to cook, when I descend the stairs with that spacey look and say in a dream-like voice, "I think I need to write something down real quick." Sorry that "real quick" usually means a couple of hours later. Thank you for all you do to help me live my dream. Thank you for crying with me when I don't know if I deserve this and for reminding me I am worthy. Thank you for your transformational love.

To my sons, Jadon, Asa, Hosea, Zadok, Boaz, and Asher—your creativity, your inspiration, your witty comments, your wonder, your joy, and your hope—they are all life-giving to me. I love you so very much.

Mom: Thank you for always believing in me and nurturing my love of both reading and writing. Thank you for keeping pencils in stock and stapling my "books" together when I was a little girl. And thank you for keeping them all.

Kervin: Thank you for adopting us as your children.

Aunt Lynette: Thank you for buying me my first writing book when I was eight. I still have it on one of my shelves.

Ashley and Jarrod: Thank you for teaching me what it means to be a sister and for sticking with me through hell and high water. You're the best siblings I could ever imagine.

Helen Montoya Henrichs: Thank you for contributing stunning photographs that helped build Paulie's story at its beginning. I am lucky to call you not only our family documentarian, but also a friend. While this story looks much different than it did in our collaborative days, you are part of its foundation. Thank you for your contribution.

Rena Rossner: Thank you for taking a chance on a cold query, for falling in love with Paulie's story and understanding just what I wanted to do with it, and for pushing me to cut and rewrite and shape it into a better book than it might have been without you. You are a master at what you do, and I'm so thankful to have such a fierce, determined, practical agent.

Sonali Fry: Thank you so very much for choosing to share Paulie's story, for seeing its potential, for shaping it into what it's become. Thank you for asking about my family, for your compassion that often made me cry (though you couldn't see it across cyberspace), for caring enough to say, "No rush, whenever you can." I am so thankful to have an editor like you.

Nic Stone: Thank you for reading an early version of this story and making some helpful suggestions. Your time is so very much appreciated.

Chris Silas Neal: Thank you for the most perfect cover of my book that I could possibly have envisioned for it—so perfect, in fact, that I cried the first time I saw it. You are amazingly gifted at what you do, and I am so honored to have a piece of your art living forever on my book.

Thank you to the entire team at Yellow Jacket: David DeWitt, Dave Barrett, Gayley Avery, and Nadia Almahdi. You have truly brought this book to life, and I will be eternally grateful for your hard work and dedication.